Exodus According to Methuselah

BOOKS BY: Reva Spiro Luxenberg

SADIE WEINSTEIN MYSTERIES
Murder at the Second Lily Pond
The Cereal Killer
Curl Up and Die
The Beauty School Murder
The Bumbling Bigamist
The Cruise Ship Murders

NOVELS
Grand Army Plaza
And Then There Was Light
A Flickering Flame
Recipe for Love

NON-FICTION
An Old Lady's Confessions
An Old Lady's Writing Tips
Native American Fun Crafts
Romantic Calligraphy

ANTHOLOGIES
The Call from Beyond
Reflections and Recollections

MODERN BIBLICAL HUMOR
Genesis According to Methuselah
Exodus According to Methuselah

Exodus According to Methuselah

Reva Spiro Luxenberg

Copyright © 2019 by Reva Spiro Luxenberg.

ISBN	Softcover	978-1-7960-3438-7
	eBook	978-1-7960-3437-0

All rights reserved. No part of this book may be reproduced or transmitted in any form or by any means, electronic or mechanical, including photocopying, recording, or by any information storage and retrieval system, without permission in writing from the copyright owner.

This is a work of fiction. Names, characters, places and incidents either are the product of the author's imagination or are used fictitiously, and any resemblance to any actual persons, living or dead, events, or locales is entirely coincidental.

Scripture quotations marked KJV are from the Holy Bible, King James Version (Authorized Version). First published in 1611. Quoted from the KJV Classic Reference Bible, Copyright © 1983 by The Zondervan Corporation.

Any people depicted in stock imagery provided by Getty Images are models, and such images are being used for illustrative purposes only.
Certain stock imagery © Getty Images.

Print information available on the last page.

Rev. date: 05/20/2019

To order additional copies of this book, contact:
Xlibris
1-888-795-4274
www.Xlibris.com
Orders@Xlibris.com
789861

INTRODUCTION

My Book *Genesis According to Methuselah* has been received with acclaim. Readers, especially my son Allen Luxenberg, urged me to write a "Methuselah" of the second book of the Bible. Since Moses is the main protagonist and I gave my son the middle name of Moses in my feeling of admiration for him, I have complied. I hope that the humor in the book doesn't offend anyone. I mean only to entertain. I might also introduce some folks to the Bible in the process.

Once again I thank my husband, Dr. Edward R. Levenson, for his devoted reading, suggestions, and skilled editing.

CHAPTER 1

IT'S ME, METHUSELAH. Oh, you don't remember who I am? So I'll remind you. I'm the grandfather of Noah, the kid who built the Ark. I was 969 years old when my wife Sheilabenautumn and I were ready to board the boat and I dropped as dead as a stone. Even though my body turned to dust, however, my soul went up to Heaven. I became the Recording Angel of History. I corrected mistakes in Genesis in my previous book *Genesis According to Methuselah*. Now I'll give you the benefit of my spectacular intelligence, deep knowledge, and superior modesty to acquaint you with the factual chronicle of what really happened during the time of Exodus. The first scribe who copied it was dyslexic and near-sighted and made as many mistakes as had happened with Genesis. Well, not quite as many because Exodus is shorter. He apparently didn't have the benefit of glasses and Special Education. So I'm resuming my correcting work with this book too.

After Jacob died, his offspring were deprived of radio, television, cars, computers, cell phones, and horse racing. To relieve the boredom, they spent a lot of time in their bedrooms. Women all over Goshen in Egypt gave birth. Many of them had twenty or more children. You can bet there were a great many crying babies.

When the babies became adults, they, of course, had more babies in turn. The land became filled with wet diapers and there was no diaper service. It was a mess! Then it became even worse when a new Pharaoh of Egypt ruled over the land. He hadn't heard about how helpful Joseph had been to the earlier Pharaoh, and he didn't care when his ministers told him about how Joseph had saved Egypt from a devastating famine.

There was a chief minister by the name of Nkosi, the meaning of which is "law and regulations." Nkosi had the ear of the Pharaoh, who relied on him for sound advice about codifying rules and policing the land.

But there was one problem that Nkosi had that made it hard for him to get his ideas across. From the time his permanent teeth had broken through his gums he had been afflicted with malocclusion. In other words his upper and lower teeth closed badly and he couldn't pronounce certain sounds.

One day when he had been awakened by the bawling of a Hebrew infant, Nkosi decided to talk to the Pharaoh. He strutted with his spindly legs through the corridors of the palace with their high-pillared halls. He strode past the rooms, apartments, and terraces until he came to the throne room. It was a room of overwhelming splendor. The royal chamber had a floor of black marble. The white linen hangings of the room, embroidered with hieroglyphics, were suspended between twenty-five foot granite columns. Behind the throne was a brick wall covered with a mosaic that depicted the Pharaoh standing in his chariot. White limestone with gold inlay covered the throne platform. The throne itself was a carved block of pale alabaster.

This morning Pharaoh sat in the attire of Ra, the sun-god. He wore the golden crown of Ra on his head. In his left hand he held the golden sickle. On his body he wore a pleated, knee-length kilt of white linen. His right palm supported his broad chin. His expression was one of boredom. Priests, clerks, and stewards stood in silence at a respectful distance around the great hall.

Nkosi approached the throne, bowed, and gave the royal salute, which was touching the fingers of both hands to his eyes. Pharaoh nodded and smiled thinly. "My Lord Goodness Gracious (Nikosi always addressed the Pharaoh that way), the Hebrews have flooded our land like red an. They are more numerous than us. If there is a war, they may join our enemies and fight against us."

Pharaoh's scalp itched. He lifted his crown and scratched his head. Then he asked, "What are 'red an'?"

"They are tiny insects that bite. The Hebrews may plot against us. Let us apply our brilliant minds and take action."

The Pharaoh nodded. "What kind of action? Should we kill all of them?"

Nkosi put his hand on his temple. "No. I have another solution. Put them to work. Not just eight hours a day fiddling around, but let them suffer under taskmasters and build the treasure cities Pithom and Rameses."

"Oooh, I like the idea of making the Hebrews suffer," Pharaoh said with an evil grin.

"Furthermore," Nkosi said, "these people and their children can read. They have a twenty-two-letter alphabet and they can write and circulate flyers that could instigate rebellion."

"Our hieroglyphs are more artistic," Pharaoh said, as he tugged at his false beard. "Only royalty, priests, and civil officials can read them. That makes us unique, outstanding, and unrivaled. The Hebrews cannot possibly communicate well against us. I'm not worried about that at all."

Nkosi felt relieved.

Pharaoh asked, "What shall the Hebrews use to construct our cities?"

"Mortar and bri, my Lord Goodness Gracious."

"What's 'bri'? You mean cheese?"

"No, certainly not cheese. I have trouble pronouncing certain letters. I'll write it out in hieroglyphs."

"Never mind," Pharaoh said, waving his arm to dismiss his chief minister. "As long as they work like dogs, I don't care what kind of materials they use."

The men of Israel suffered under the cruel taskmasters and the only relief they had was at night when they went home to their caring wives. The women tended to their husbands' bruises and cuts, they fed them nourishing meals, and they were solicitous of their physical needs. As a result the Hebrews multiplied—even more than before. The land became completely filled with crying babies—babies who drooled, dribbled, and crawled all over Upper and Lower Egypt.

The main industry in Egypt was farming, especially along the river Nile. The mothers had so many babies they couldn't keep an eye on all of them, and the toddlers took to picking out carrots, potatoes, and squash haphazardly. This came to the attention of Nkosi, who made an unscheduled appointment to see the king.

CHAPTER 2

THE NEXT DAY at noon Chief Minister Nkosi was ushered into the Pharaoh's presence. There were flies all over the throne and stewards were batting them with fly swatters fashioned out of lotus leaves.

"I cannot stand these annoying flies," Pharaoh said. "Do you have a solution for getting rid of them, Nkosi?"

Nkosi was a wise man and after a troubled silence he came up with an answer. "My Lord Goodness Gracious, if you stop eating at your throne and eat in the dining room instead, the flies will remain in the dining room and your throne will be free of these flies."

Pharaoh clapped his hands. "You are indeed a clever man. Why haven't I thought of that? But why have you sought my attention? Is there a problem in my kingdom?"

"Yes, my Lord Goodness Gracious. The Hebrew children are destroying our vegetable gardens. Furthermore, believe it or not, the Hebrews continue to multiply just like the an." (Remember I told you that Nkosi had a speech impediment.)

"The what?"

"You know the 'an', the insect that makes 'an' hills."

"Oh, yes. Go on, I haven't got all day. I have to inspect my troops."

Nkosi wiped off the perspiration from under his bulbous nose. "My Lord Goodness Gracious, my plan is to get rid of all the newborn males. The population of the Hebrews will thus decrease to a reasonable size."

"Great idea," the king said. "How should we do that?"

Nkosi smiled with a huge smile that showed his crooked and black teeth. When he remembered that he shouldn't display his ugly teeth, he put his hand over his mouth and spoke "De midwiv . . ."

Pharaoh interrupted. "Take your hand away from your mouth so I can understand what you are saying."

"Yes, my Lord Goodness Gracious. Order the midwives, 'When you deliver a son you are to kill him. You may spare a daughter.'"

"I will speak to only two," Pharaoh said. "I get nervous when large groups come before me. Just find two and send them to my throne room. I will return when the sun is overhead."

Nkosi nodded. "I will send you Puah and Shiphrah. They deliver more babies than any other midwives. They have been trained by Dinah, the elder midwife who never lost a baby. I call them P.S."

That's how "P.S." originated. People think it's from "*post scriptum*" which means "written after," if you don't happen to know because you never took Latin in high school; but it had been a biblical derivation before that.

The plan was feasible and clever, but not clever enough because the midwives feared the Lord and wouldn't murder anyone. And thus the Hebrew population continued to grow. Pharaoh's wife was gorgeous, but she was also a mean and cunning woman. Mrs. Pharaoh had only two children and declined to have any more since she was vain and didn't want to spoil her glamorous figure. She also had a phobia known as misophonia, that is, a hatred of repetitive sounds. She couldn't eat dinner with her husband because the sound of his chewing, especially when he chomped down on celery, set her off. She felt intense anxiety that turned into panic and then rage. Then she went on a rampage and smashed all the dishes. Sweat poured down her body and into her sandals. Her blood pressure soared sky high.

The palace walls weren't soundproof and the wails of the Hebrew infants reached the sensitive ears of Mrs. Pharaoh. She rushed into the throne room and confronted her husband. For a minute she watched as the massage servant removed the king's Nemes crown and was starting to give the Pharaoh a soothing massage on his bare head.

"Rammy," Mrs. Pharaoh yelled. "Rammy" was the name she called her husband when she was disturbed. Otherwise she referred to him as "Ram" or "Sweet Date." "Rammy, we have to get rid of all these Hebrew babies, or I shall die of a stroke."

Pharaoh dismissed his massage servant and replaced his Nemes crown. "I have already spoken to the P.S. midwives and they assured me that they will kill the male infants."

Mrs. Pharaoh stamped her foot so hard she collapsed on her throne and called for help. "Servant woman, bring me a bowl of ice to relieve my pain."

An elderly woman brought her a bowl of rice. Mrs. Pharaoh screamed, "I said 'ice' not 'rice.'" The servant ran to the kitchen and brought back a solid block of ice. Mrs. Pharaoh placed her foot on the ice and heaved a sigh of relief. Then she changed the servant's job to that of toilet cleaner.

But when the ice started to break apart, it made crackling sounds that sent Mrs. Pharaoh into another rage. Furthermore, Pharaoh's wife heard another repetitive noise. Her husband was biting down on a date pit. He liked dates and that's why when Mrs. Pharaoh was in a loving mood she called her husband "Sweet Date." Mrs. Pharaoh stumbled from the throne room, raced into her private suite, threw herself down on her bed, and put her fingers in her ears. Then she began to bawl like an infant.

Pharaoh took the pit out of his mouth and ran to comfort his beautiful wife. "Sweet rose of my heart," he said, ". . . I shall talk to the midwives again and this time they will listen to me or else."

Mrs. Pharaoh took her fingers out of her ears. "What did you say?"

"I said the midwives will listen to me or else there will be no more midwives."

"Sweet Date, if there are no more midwives, the Hebrew women will deliver their own babies."

Pharaoh wrinkled his forehead. "I hadn't thought of that. Still and all, I will speak harshly to them."

CHAPTER 3

THE HEBREW MIDWIVES Puah and Shiphrah were summoned to the throne room. Pharaoh had a date pit in his mouth. He removed it and said, "Why haven't you listened to me and why are you saving the male infants? You better have a good reason, or I will have you hanged."

They came prepared to appease the king with a logical answer. It had taken them fifteen hours to think of this clever excuse. "Majesty, the Hebrew women don't take as long as the Egyptian women to give birth. They are used to having many children and, as everyone knows, it takes them less time for labor with every birth. By the time we get to the women they have already delivered. All we have to do is cut the umbilical cords."

"I'll have to think about this," the Pharaoh said. "Meanwhile there is something else you can do."

"Yes, Your Majesty, we wish to please you," they both said with the sweetest of smiles.

"My wife is very sensitive to the cries of the babies. Can you stop their crying?"

Shiphrah spoke, "We can definitely do that."

Puah said, "If you will give us black grapes, we shall make wine. We will coat the babies' tongues with the wine. It will sedate them and they will stop crying. We guarantee it."

The Pharaoh nodded. He was very pleased about this turn of events. Now his super-sensitive, complaining wife wouldn't give him a hard time.

#

Even though the wine worked wonders, however, the population of the Hebrew male babies continued to increase. The carriage industry thrived as did the manufacture of diapers. The land became so crowded that the builders had to add stories to the floors and additions to the houses. If you think that India, Japan, or China are crowded, you should have seen Goshen, where five Hebrews had to sleep in the same bed and four babies had to share one crib.

When Mrs. Pharaoh heard that the male Hebrew baby population was increasing steadily, she rushed to her husband's side. As soon as he saw her, he spit out the date pit. He hated when she yelled at him about the noise he made when biting on date pits. "Rammy, you have no choice but to kill all the male Hebrew babies by throwing them into our sacred river Nile."

"What about the girls? What shall we do about the girls?"

"Girls don't go to war, so you can let them live. Besides, they make good servants and they are thorough furniture dusters in the palace."

And so it came to pass that many, many Hebrew male infants were drowned. However, there was a man by the name of Amram Levi of the house of Levi who married Yocheved, who was also of the house of Levi. It was convenient for a Levite man to marry a woman of the same tribe. They had a big wedding and a lot of dancing and such loud music that Mrs. Pharaoh complained bitterly. She sent guards to the wedding to order that the music be stopped.

When the music had stopped and all the food had been consumed, the newlyweds went to bed. That evening, believe it or not, Yocheved became pregnant. Amram and Yocheved were a no-nonsense couple.

Nine months to the day a daughter was born to the happy Levis. They named her Miriam. Seven years later they had a son who they named Aaron. On the very same day, three years later, February 17[th,] another son was born. When they became adults, both sons celebrated their birthday together. Their common birthday helped them bond.

One thing, of course, spoiled the parents' joy. They were fearful that their baby would be thrown into the river. Yocheved, who was not only attractive but wise, was able to hide him by taking the advice of the midwives. Every time the baby started to cry she put a few drops of wine on his tongue, and he stopped crying and smiled with pleasure. Month after month this worked. But in the third month the baby refused to open his mouth for the drops of wine because he was concentrating on sitting up. He didn't succeed in this endeavor so quickly, but that didn't prevent him from trying to observe the world around him.

When baby Levi was three months old, Mrs. Yocheved Levi realized that he was too old to conceal. It was on a Sunday in April right after dinner when she said to her husband. "Our baby cries loudly every once in a while and the Egyptian guards will hear him and kill him. I can't keep him quiet any longer."

"Put our baby in a basket," Amram said, ". . . and put the basket in the river and the good Lord God will send someone to rescue him."

Yocheved answered in a puzzled way, "I don't have a basket."

"Make one," Amram said. "I'd do it myself but the Egyptians keep me busy all day making mudbricks."

Pharaoh had set aside the land of Goshen for the Hebrews because the Egyptians refused to live there. Goshen didn't occupy a large area, but it was grassy most of the time except when it flooded occasionally. When the land flooded, as it had done a month before, the soil which was rich in good clay couldn't be ploughed. Harvests were meager, and people had little to eat. They had access to the River Nile, however, and were able to fish.

Yocheved crept down to the Nile at midnight to gather a bundle of bulrushes to make the basket. It wasn't easy for her to pull the reeds from the marshy ground on the banks of the river. She staggered home stealthily carrying the heavy burden of bulrushes. Then she cut the fiber of each one to make strips.

The next morning Yocheved took all the strips and hid them behind a wall of stones that she had built. When the sun shone brightly, the strips dried. She made sure before she sewed the strips together that there was no moisture on them. When Yocheved attempted to thread a bone needle with a strip, she had a hard time. "Oy vey," she moaned, "Inserting a strip through a tiny hole is tough." She worked hard, spitting on each one to make it more pliable. In olden days needle threaders hadn't yet been invented. You have to give Yocheved credit for her perseverance in the face of adversity.

The next step was measuring the length of her baby, which took ten minutes because he squirmed around a lot. Then Yocheved sat down at her kitchen table to design the shape of the small basket.

When the baby started to cry, Yocheved stopped what she was doing and nursed him. After he fell asleep, she went back to her painstaking work.

Sewing the strips together took two weeks. Then Yocheved went to the river bank. She located a pine tree and extracted pitch with a spoon she had brought from her kitchen. She needed it to seal the basket. She also gathered enough slime to act as a seal as well. Slime is a lustrous black solid that the Egyptians used in embalming their mummies. Her neighbor who worked in the palace had given her this secret information, which had really become common knowledge and wasn't a secret anymore. Even in biblical times it was known that once you reveal a secret the cat is out of the bag.

Yocheved smeared the pitch and the slime all over the basket, inside and outside. She waited until it dried. Another week passed before her red and raw hands came clean after scrubbing them. It's my opinion as Methuselah that even though Amram labored making bricks for the Pharaoh, Yocheved worked just as hard.

The whole process took a month. By now the baby was no longer three months old as it is written in Exodus. I told you there are mistakes that I have to correct. The baby boy was going on five months and he could sit up and look around.

Yocheved waited until her son was sleeping and then she put him into the basket. She asked her ten-year-old daughter Miriam to accompany her. Miriam was the kind of kid who listened to requests without giving any backtalk like the kids of today.

Gently, and with tears in her eyes, Yocheved carried the basket to the bank of the river and laid it down among the reeds.

Suddenly the baby sat up and began to cry as he looked at the river and realized this wasn't familiar. Yocheved picked him up and rocked him in her arms until he fell asleep again.

"Miriam," Yocheved said in a teary voice, ". . . you stay here, not too close, about four cubits away, and watch what happens to your brother. I'm going home because my heart is breaking."

After two hours of standing Miriam became weary and sat down by the river's edge. She lay back cushioned by the reeds and fell asleep. Suddenly, she heard a noise that awakened her. Egyptian maidens were laughing and conversing in loud voices and lo and behold, she saw the Princess, the daughter of the Pharaoh herself. The Princess had attractive features but she looked forlorn. Miriam, with sweat running down her back, patted down her hair, brushed off some of the reeds from her robe, and from a distance watched the Princess remove her clothing and bathe in the river.

Miriam was shocked when she saw the nude Princess—not from her nakedness but from what was on her body. Inflamed raised lesions covered by silvery scales were on her back. Miriam bit down on her lips to prevent her from crying out. A feeling of compassion overwhelmed her. I, Methuselah, know that in modern times we call the condition the poor Princess was afflicted with plaque psoriasis, but at that time no one knew anything about this. Even so the Princess had been advised by the Chief Physician to bathe in the holy Nile River and she faithfully followed his advice.

When the Princess was covered with water up to her neck, she heard a baby crying. She sent her maid servant to investigate.

The woman brought back a basket. Inside was a baby sitting up and whimpering. The Princess looked with intense curiosity at this infant who she surmised was a Hebrew. She knew her father had ordered all male Hebrew newborns to be killed, but how did this child survive? The baby stopped crying and looked at her. He had straight black hair and was quite cute. She smiled to him, and he smiled right back, and put up his chubby hands to be picked up. The Princess was an animal lover. She had twenty cats, and the baby was no cat, but she fell in love with his warm smile. She wondered if she could take him back to the palace and raise him as her own.

The maidens took the baby away from her and then dried her with a large linen towel. In those days fluffy cotton Turkish towels hadn't yet been invented. After the Princess had gotten dressed, Miriam, with her legs shaking with fear, approached her and asked, "Your Royal Highness, are you going to keep this child?"

"I don't know," the Princess said, as the baby took hold of her finger. "He's adorable."

Miriam took a step forward. "I know of a Hebrew woman who could nurse him for you. Shall I call her?"

The Princess Hatshepsut held the baby close in her arms. He cooed and smiled up at her. "Yes, go ask her to come. I'm keeping this baby even if my father forbids it. I'll change his mind."

CHAPTER 4

MIRIAM RACED HOME to her sun-dried brick house with the amazing news that the Princess wanted to keep her baby brother. "*Imma,*" she said, "The Princess wants you to nurse the baby and I think she'll pay you."

"Wow," Yocheved said.

Miriam's eyes lit up. "We'll be rich!"

Yocheved put her hand on her forehead. "I don't care about the money. I care about the miracle that God has wrought."

Now if you think that the Princess hadn't realized that Yocheved was indeed the new baby's mother, you have no idea how clever she was. She had been thinking deeply. *How come that young girl was in the right place at the right time? How did she know of a wet-nurse?* If you haven't figured this out by now, I suggest, as Methuselah, that you should give up the idea of becoming a private eye.

When Yocheved put in her first appearance in the palace, the Princess said, "I have named the baby 'Moses' since it means 'drawn from the river.' I know you're the real mother and that's all right with me. He can address you as 'Mama.' I will be his mother, too. He can call me 'Mother Princess.' You may teach him the language and the religion of the Hebrews. We will all share this secret. I personally believe all our gods are created by your God, but since I don't want to make waves, I keep my thoughts to myself. Moses will also be taught everything Egyptian including our religion. Is that all right with you?"

As soon as Yocheved heard the beginning of the Princess's words, she fainted and didn't hear the part about the Princess accepting her belief in one God or that Moses would be exposed to Egyptian beliefs. She was relieved that her son would be safe.

The Princess brought her new son to her father in his private chamber. "I have an ugly skin condition," she told the Pharaoh. "I won't ever get married, but I want to be a mother." She lifted the blanket that was wrapped around Moses.

Pharaoh peered at the baby. "Is that child a Hebrew?"

"Yes, he is. His spirit has worked its way into my heart. Please, Father, let me keep him."

Pharaoh's eyes bulged. "Do you think I'd let a Hebrew live in my palace? My subjects would revolt and make mud of me."

"But father, you don't have to tell the truth. The baby looks just like an Egyptian."

"You want me to lie? I am not only a Pharaoh, but I am a god. Gods don't lie."

The princess took a breath. "I'm not asking you to lie. If you say nothing about the baby, no one will know or suspect. They'll think he's Egyptian."

"My good-hearted daughter, will this baby be raised as an Egyptian?"

"Of course. He'll learn the Egyptian language and religion. I promise you I'll raise him to be an Egyptian prince and you'll be very proud of him."

"Have you given him a name?"

The Princess climbed the steps of the throne and planted a kiss on her father's cheek. "Yes, father. I named him 'Moses,' because I drew him from the water."

When Pharaoh heard that his daughter had given the boy an Egyptian name, his heart melted and he agreed to let her keep the child.

The Levi family moved closer to the palace so Yocheved could be available for her nursing job every four hours. She began to teach her son blessings over different foods and drinks. Moses as you can imagine, was very smart, and he grasped the unusual situation he was in. He started to learn Hebrew and Egyptian at the same time and he became bilingual at a very young age.

One day Yocheved cast an admiring look at her nine-month-old baby. He was on the floor sitting up and holding on to one of the legs of the kitchen table. Suddenly he pulled himself up and began to walk with unsteady steps. "Miriam, come here," Yocheved called to her daughter, who was in the next room. "See what Moses is doing!"

Miriam gasped. "I can't believe the baby is walking. How old was I when I walked?"

"You were thirteen months, and first you crawled. He never crawled."

The following month Moses said in Hebrew, *"Boker tov."*

Aaron spoke to his brother, "What did you say?"

"I said *'boker tov'!*"

"Imma," Aaron said in an excited voice. "My baby brother just said 'good morning.' He's only ten months old. He must be a genius."

Moses' developmental milestones were so remarkable they threatened Pharaoh and Pharaoh sent for Chief Minister Nkosi. "There's something about Moses that threatens me. He's so brilliant and has developed so fast that he may try to murder me and take the throne for himself. Do you have any suggestion to allay my worries?"

Nkosi scratched his head. "Put the toddler to a test. Give the boy your crown. If he puts it on his head, then you should kill him since it will prove he'll want to take your throne from you. But if he doesn't, then you can let him live in peace in the palace."

"What a wonderful idea," Pharaoh said. "Let's not waste any more time. Bring him in and we'll see what happens."

Nkosi carried the boy in his arms. Moses could tell by the perspiration on Nkosi's face that he was up to something. Taking small hurried steps, Nkosi entered the throne room. "I've brought you the child, My Lord Goodness Gracious," Nkosi said as he put Moses down on the marble floor. Then he bowed and put his hands on his closed eyes to show reverence for Pharaoh.

With a scowl on his face, Pharaoh removed his crown. Moses wondered what he was up to. Pharaoh stepped down from his throne, bent down, and held out his crown to Moses who took it in his hands. Moses had been taught by both his princess mother and biological mother to say 'thank you' when given something. He nodded as he held the crown and in a child's high voice he murmured, "Thank you." He took the crown and bit into it using it as a pacifier like babies do today. Pharaoh took it away in cold surprise as a servant grabbed a piece of linen and thoroughly cleaned it from the child's saliva. Moses was astute and had passed the test with flying colors.

Pharaoh still wasn't satisfied. That night he dreamed he saw Moses sitting on his throne. He awoke at dawn and sent for his chief minister. Nkosi had to dress hurriedly. He knocked at the door of Pharaoh's royal chamber. "Enter," Pharaoh called out. He himself hadn't yet dressed and put on his makeup. He looked just like any other man.

"You sent for me, My Lord Goodness Gracious. I am at your service."

"I had a nightmare that Moses sat on my throne," Pharaoh said, sitting up in his royal bed with embroidered linen pillows and fancy coverlet. "I need you to devise another test for the boy so that I can be at peace."

"I need time to think. May I return when the sun is directly overhead, Your Majesty?"

"You may go but make sure when you return the test you will devise is faultless."

Nkosi spoke to his wife about the problem of coming up with a test that the Pharaoh would accept. Mrs. Nkosi was a calculating woman. She cocked an ear, listened to her husband, and nodded. "I am acquainted with children since we have eight. I have just the thing to satisfy Pharaoh."

Nkosi returned and took credit for his wife's plan. He said, "My Lord Goodness Gracious, I have devised a test that is infallible. We'll give Moses a cup of hot cocoa. If he sticks his finger in it to see if it's cool enough to drink, then we'll know he can be a dangerous threat to your crown."

When the hot cocoa was brought to Moses, he smelled it and drank it. "Ouch," he cried, as he burned his tongue.

Afterwards, as a result, it was difficult for him to pronounce words correctly. Moses was so brilliant that he knew he had had to drink the hot cocoa to fool his step-grandfather. This change in Moses brought about a complete transformation in Nkosi's feelings about Moses, for both Nkosi and Moses now had the same speech defect.

One day Pharaoh confided to Nkosi, "I will tell you a secret and if you reveal it, I will have you hanged by your neck. Do you promise to keep this secret?"

"I do. I swear by Osiris that I will not betray you, My Lord Goodness Gracious."

"All right then. Here it goes. Moses is a Hebrew."

Nikosi turned as white as a hard-cooked egg. "He is?"

"Yes, my daughter found him in a basket in the Nile."

There was a strained silence until Nkosi spoke, "My Lord Goodness Gracious, I shall keep your secret. You can rely on me."

#

Two moons later, even though Moses had passed the second test, Pharaoh's sleep was still disturbed. He dreamed that Moses was in cahoots with his enemies. He called for his chief minister. "I want you to give the boy a test that is so severe it will convince me that he is harmless."

All color drained from Nkosi's face. *Will my wife be able to help me devise another foolproof test? I can't think of anything off the bat. Woe is me!*

In the beginning when Nkosi learned that Moses was a Hebrew not only had he disliked him but he had hated him. Now the situation was reversed considering that after Moses burned his tongue and his speech became affected, he sounded just like him. He had kept it a secret that Moses was a Hebrew, even though he wanted to reveal the truth to his wife, but his loyalty to Pharaoh wouldn't let him. Nkosi's heart had softened when he listened to Moses talking with halting speech and suffering in doing so. But now faced with a dilemma, he was a nervous wreck. How could they devise a test that would both satisfy Pharaoh and not hurt Moses? It took a week for his wife to come up with one.

"I came up with a most brilliant plan," Mrs. Nkosi bragged.

"Quick, tell me what it is?"

"Moses will be submerged in the Nile and not drown."

"What?" Nkosi cried out. "That's impossible."

"No, it isn't. He will breathe through a hollowed-out reed."

"Sweetie pie," Nkosi said. "Do you think there's any possibility that the child might drown just the same?"

"Don't be ridiculous. If you follow my directions, he will be saved. You can tell Pharaoh that the plan is yours. Of course, I expect a gift from you for the prolonged thinking I did to save your position."

"I will buy you whatever your heart desires. What do you want?"

"I have longed for a necklace of lapis lazuli diamond-shaped beads."

"I will get such a necklace for you."

Mrs. Nkosi placed her hand on her forehead. "I also want earrings and a ring to match."

"Yes, sweetie pie. You deserve such jewelry to complement your lovely looks."

I, Methuselah, know for a fact that Mrs. Nkosi bulged with fat, and that a necklace would enhance the rolls of fat on her neck but she, of course, didn't realize this.

Nkosi searched for the widest reed that grew along the Nile. He hollowed it out. Then he took Moses into the privacy of his room and said, "When the time comes and you will be submerged in the Nile, you should breathe through the reed."

"I don't like getting my hair wet in the dirty river," Moses said.

"Do you want Pharaoh to kill you?"

Moses bit down on his lips. "I don't want anyone to kill me."

"Then listen to me. Getting your hair wet is the least of your worries. You must rely on the reed to breathe fresh air."

"Well, if I have to, I will."

After Moses agreed, Nkosi approached Pharaoh with the test.

"My Lord Goodness Gracious," he said, "I propose such a difficult test that it will surely confirm that Moses is no threat to you."

Pharaoh's jaw dropped. "That's what I've been waiting for. Hurry, tell me what it is."

"The head security guard, who is trustworthy, will take Moses to the Nile and submerge him under water for a count of nine hundred. If Moses doesn't drown, it will prove that his God looks after him. We won't be guilty of killing him, but Moses will see that you do have the authority to do so. He'll be frightened and never attempt to take away your crown. At any rate, you don't have anything to worry about. Moses' God won't ever want him to become a Pharaoh, as his God isn't in competition with you, My Lord Goodness Gracious. And if, however, he would die, so be it."

"That's a brilliant plan," Pharaoh said. "It's possible that he'll drown and then I'll be free of him. But we must do this without my daughter knowing, since Moses is her adopted son and she's very attached to him. I will send for my chief guard to do the deed."

The Chief Security Guard Sabra (the name meaning "patient" in Egyptian) stood in silence, his chest heaving as Pharaoh ordered him to bring a boy child to the Nile. "You are to submerge him and count to nine hundred before bringing him up."

Sabra's heart hammered in his chest. "Your Royal Majesty, I shall do as you command. But I do not know how to count to nine hundred."

Pharaoh's face darkened. He cried harshly, "You are to go to my chief mathematician and learn all the numbers in one day. Do you understand?"

"I understand, Your Royal Majesty. I shall learn how to count to nine hundred."

Two days later Sabra picked the child up and carried him to the Nile. Moses didn't utter a sound. He had the reed in a pocket of his linen robe and Moses knew he would survive this difficult trial. But prior to being dunked, Moses small hands smacked and flicked at the river gnats that were biting him.

Sabra said, "It's all right. The bugs won't bite you under the water." Then when Sabra cast Moses into the river, tears flowed down the guard's face as he was convinced that the child would die. He had two young sons and as he thought about a boy dying in this way he was stricken with grief. Sabra kept crying as he pushed Moses down. His tears prevented him from seeing the reed that Moses had put in his mouth. Sabra counted one, two, three until he reached nine hundred. Moses kept calm as he was able to breathe the warm air.

When Sabra lifted Moses out of the river, the child began to cry. Sabra's heart pounded with shock. He let out his breath in a long tortured sigh.

After Pharaoh was notified of the outcome, he relaxed when he realized that Moses wasn't a threat. From then on both Nkosi and Sabra took an active interest in caring for and educating Moses.

Moses moved back and forth from the palace to his home with his biological parents, who kept teaching him the Hebrew language and their religious practices. Once he came home and said, "The Nile where Princess Mother found me is a god."

Yocheved replied, "No, my son. The Egyptians believe in many gods, but we Hebrews believe in only one."

"That makes sense," Moses said.

His mother taught him many important principles like when she said, "Remember never pay retail."

"What does 'retail' mean?" Moses asked.

"You'll find out," Yocheved answered. "Now I want to teach you how to sew."

"That's not necessary," Moses said. "We have many tailors in the palace."

Yocheved shook her head. "You won't be living in the palace all your life. Knowing how to sew is a very useful skill." She threaded a needle and showed Moses how to make a strong backstitch on linen.

"I like sewing," Moses said, after he had quickly picked up the skill. "Maybe I should become a tailor."

"You're meant for bigger things, my son," his mother said, as she showed him how to make a knot.

When they finished sewing, Yocheved fed him her noodle pudding with dates. "Eat! Eat, my boy! You need strength to worry!"

A thin slave by the name of Meyer was the one who held Moses in his arms as he gave the child his first camel ride. "How do you feel riding a camel?" Meyer asked.

"I'm feeling sick," Moses said. "I like being high, but I think I have motion sickness. Please tell the camel to lower his legs and I'll get off."

Nowadays youngsters are taught how to drive a car, but in biblical times the first transportation was with camels. Years later Moses learned how to drive a chariot and for some unknown reason he didn't suffer from motion sickness. Chariots were used for warfare, but they didn't cause nearly as many accidents as cars now do.

Moses was nine years old when he designed a soft cushion to sit on while riding a camel or for comfort in a chariot. He stuffed the cushion with goose down and he used the strong backstitch to sew the sides. He showed his cushion to people in the palace and they were impressed. He made many more cushions and distributed them as gifts.

Sabra waited until Moses was ten years old to teach him how to defend himself. The Chief Security Guard was the inventor of boxing gloves. Also he was instrumental in setting the rules that are still in use today. Every day except weekends he gave Moses boxing lessons in the small room adjacent to the throne room in the court. Moses paid close attention to Sabra's words. "You will learn how to jab, cross, hook, uppercut, slip, and duck. But first I'll show you the proper stance."

Moses was skinny, but he was strong even when he was ten. Sabra said, "Stand with your feet shoulder-width apart. You're left-handed, so take one step back with your left foot."

Moses tried this. "No," Sabra said, "Keep your left toe in line with your right heel and bend your knees for agility."

Moses did as he was instructed.

"Now you have good balance," Sabra said with a smile. "With this position you can use your hips for power when you throw a punch. Now inhale to prepare for throwing that hard punch. Go ahead now!"

Moses took a deep breath and let his hand, which was encased in a small boxing glove, fly forward.

"No," Sabra said. "Exhale fast through your mouth with a closed jaw. This sounds like the hiss a rattlesnake makes. The sharp exhale is to match the punch with timing and power. Try it again."

Moses was a fast learner. This time he did it right. Sabra patted him on his shoulder and smiled his approval. "Now I'll teach you to jab. Take your boxing stance. Quickly extend your arm straight out the same time you step forward with your right front foot. I'll demonstrate."

Moses watched with intense interest as Sabra moved fast with a jab. He also pulled back in a second. "You see," Sabra said, ". . . this is the quickest punch that uses the least amount of energy."

"Teach me more," Moses said.

"Tomorrow. It's too much for you to absorb in one day. Now go to your chamber and practice."

CHAPTER 5

NKOSI TOOK AN active interest in acquainting Moses with Egyptian life. He strolled with Moses around the numerous gardens and pointed out the chrysanthemums and lotus leaves that covered the many pools. The sun lit up everything in sight and cast shadows on the water. Moses was amused by the sunlight-dancing motes of dust and he concentrated his eyes on them.

Another day Nkosi showed Moses the paintings that hung displayed on the palace walls. "Aren't they beautiful," he asked.

"Yes," Moses said. "They warm my heart. I shall come back and copy the one of Pharaoh seated on his throne."

"You like to draw?" Nkosi asked.

"I do. I would like to learn how to paint."

Nkosi opened his eyes wide. "Then I shall send one of the best artists to teach you." That was the start of one of Moses' hobbies.

Another time Nkosi told Moses, "Always keep in mind that Egypt, known as 'Tamerech', will either become great and greater or fall to ashes. We are a country with many enemies. You must learn about warfare so that our country will rise up in glory."

Nkosi brought young boys to play games with Moses. The games were mostly violent simulations of warfare and Moses learned his lessons well.

"Pharaoh doesn't put me on his knee," Moses complained.

"You aren't his son, so it's not appropriate," Nkosi said. "I'll put you on my knee because I like you very much." Nkosi sat down on a bench and placed Moses on his knee. "Are you comfortable?" he asked.

"Yes, Great Vizier," Moses said. "I like you too."

"In my chamber I have a white robe for you to put on. There's a gold band for your waist, and from this band hangs an ankh made of gold."

"What's an 'ankh'?" Moses asked.

"An ankh is a symbol for 'the key of life.' It's a cross with a loop at the top. The symbol is a hieroglyph for 'life' or 'breath of life.' We believe in the afterlife. Now I'll take you to my chamber and dress you in religious attire. We'll go to the temple and pray. In the temple we wear no sandals. You'll go barefoot."

"I'll go wherever you want me to go and get dressed anyway you want me to," Moses said in his attempt to please the vizier. With his hand he touched his black hair that was cut straight across his brow. *I like Nkosi. He has become my true friend.*

"Have you had your morning meal?" Nkosi asked.

"Yes. I had fish and blood of the Nile."

"Good boy," Nkosi said, as he patted Moses on the head. "Instead of saying 'water', you are right to call it 'blood of the Nile.' Do you know the name of the god of the Nile?"

"Not yet," Moses said politely.

"The god of the Nile is called '*Hapi.*' Repeat after me, '*Hapi*.'"

"*Hapi*. He is the god of the Nile. It sounds like this god is happy. Is he happy?"

"Yes, of course he's happy because when the Nile overflows farmers use the water for irrigation. Without the Nile there wouldn't be food in Egypt."

"I'll remember that," Moses said.

Nkosi was pleased. "You will learn many lessons from the *Book of the Dead*."

"I will study it and memorize everything in it. Is there a *Book of the Living*?"

"No. Why do you ask?"

"Because someday I think I would like to write the *Book of the Living*," Moses said emphatically. "Now I'm hungry. Shall we eat food at mid-day?"

"No, we eat no food at mid-day, but after sunset you and I will eat fish, herbs from our land, and blood of the vine."

"Thank you, Great Vizier." *Imma told me that I should not accept false Egyptian gods. We Hebrews believe in the one God who is our Creator. But I have to listen to Nkosi and do as he says. Imma says there's much Egyptian wisdom that will be helpful for me to learn.*

The next day, which was the third day of the second month, not only did Moses have another lesson in boxing, but Nkosi took him outside the palace. Nkosi put the child on his one-horse chariot and they raced through the desert with the horse kicking up sand. "Are you afraid?" Nkosi asked.

"No, there is nothing to be afraid of, Great Vizier. I like to see the outside. I like the way horses race. I would like to race on a horse."

"After the Nile rises twelve times, I'll teach you to ride a horse. I'm proud of your courage."

"Thank you, Great Vizier. I hope I won't have motion sickness on a horse."

"Why do you say that?"

Moses bit down on his teeth. "Once I suffered motion sickness on a camel, but I did get over it."

Nkosi laughed. "Riding a camel is bumpy. A horse gives you a smooth ride. By the way, do you know the name of this city?"

"I think so. It's called 'Memphis'."

Nkosi nodded. "Do you know the chief deity of Memphis?"

Moses shook his head. "No."

"His name is 'Ptak'."

"I will remember *Ptak*." *I have to remember everything that I am taught. Hapi is the god of the Nile. Ptak is the god of Memphis.*

CHAPTER 6

A SPECIAL OCCASION for the Levi family was coming up in two weeks. Moses' sister Miriam was now twenty and she was looking forward to marrying in the spring. Aaron, who was thirteen, was taking on adult religious responsibilities. Moses was ten and he and Aaron had the same birthday.

One day when the sun peeked behind a cloud Moses and Nkosi strolled in the garden. "I have a favor to ask you," Moses said, as they sat down on a bench.

"It must be something special as you never asked me for a favor before."

"My brother and I have the same birthday. I'd like to celebrate with my Hebrew family in the palace, and I'm afraid to ask Pharaoh if he would permit it. Could you ask him for me, since no Hebrews are allowed inside the palace?"

"This isn't a big favor you're asking. Of course I'll be happy to do it. Look at the sky. The cloud has passed away and the sun shines brightly. That's a good omen."

Nkosi combed his hair, washed his face, and entered the throne room. "My Lord, Goodness Gracious," he said to the Pharaoh, who was scratching his head. "Prince Moses wants to know if you'll allow his family to celebrate his birthday in the palace."

Pharaoh scrunched up his face. "I don't make exceptions for birthdays. No Hebrews are to set foot in my palace. That is my decision and it's final!"

Nkosi backed out of the throne room and immediately went home to ask his wife her opinion. Mrs. Nkosi was in the bedroom dressed in a new cranberry red frock. She was putting on the lapis lazuli beaded necklace her husband had given her as a reward for the plan that had saved Moses' life. "Sweetie Pie, you look scrumptious," Nkosi said. "The necklace accentuates your dark hair."

"What do you want now?" Mrs. Nkosi asked, as she added the ring to her stubby finger.

"It's not much of a problem. I would appreciate your helping me to solve a problem with your brilliant mind. Moses wants to have a birthday party in the palace and invite some Hebrew friends to join him. Pharaoh is against this. Can you think of any way to change his mind?"

Mrs. Nkosi pursed her lips as she added the lapis lazuli bracelet to her wrist, which was already covered with two gold bracelets. "Yes, there is a way. If I tell you how to solve this problem, what will you then give me?"

"What do you want, Sweetie Pie?"

Mrs. Nkosi rested her double chin in her hand. "I would like a ruby necklace to match this dress."

"Don't you have enough jewelry already?" *If I'm not careful, she'll eat me out of house and home and I'll wind up selling dates.*

"Mr. Karim isn't a skin-flint. His wife Jomana has so much jewelry it's piled up like a tower."

Nkosi tugged at his beard. "At this juncture I really can't afford to pay for more jewelry, Sweetie Pie."

Mrs. Nkosi grunted. "I will give you clever advice that you asked for, and you won't reward me?"

"No! I'm sure it's great advice. But for now isn't there anything else you'd like instead?"

Mrs. Nkosi's eyes widened. "All right. I would like to invite the Karims over for a luxurious dinner and we'll hire the best entertainment in all of Egypt. I'll wear my jewelry and a new dress that I expect you to buy."

"Well all right, Sweetie Pie. You drive a hard bargain. Now tell me your advice."

"Tell the Pharaoh that's he's absolutely right. No dirty Hebrews should set foot in the palace."

"That's not a solution, Sweetie Pie."

Mrs. Nkosi stamped her foot and went into one of her rages yelling, "My mother told me not to marry a stupid man. I should've taken her advice."

Nkosi, with a long face and dejected expression, left his house and raced back to the palace. This time he wouldn't listen to his wife. She didn't know that Moses was not only a Hebrew but that he was a child who had found favor not only in the Princess' eyes but in his eyes as well.

He knocked loudly at the Princess's door.

"Who is it?" her servant called out.

"It's the Chief Vizier come to see the Princess."

A diminutive servant girl opened the door. "The Princess asks for you to wait in the outer room until she comes out."

Nkosi paced around the room. It was decorated with paintings of horses, dogs, and cats. He waited a long time until the Princess stepped into the room. She smiled at him. "Nkosi, this is the first time you've honored me with your presence in my quarters. How can I help you?"

"Your Royal Highness. I come to ask a favor concerning your adopted son."

"Moses?"

"Yes."

"Moses has a birthday coming up and he wants to make a party in the palace and invite his family, but your father has told me he won't permit it. Perhaps if you asked him, he would listen to his loving daughter."

"My father has a closed mind. It simply won't work."

Nkosi sighed. "My wife always says that you never know something until you try it. She's a pretty clever lady."

"Did she advise you to come to me and ask for my help?"

Nkosi put his hand to his mouth and coughed. "Not exactly—but if you tell your father that this will be only once—maybe he'll change his mind."

"How do you know Moses won't want to have a party again with his family when he's eleven, or twelve, or sixteen?"

"I don't know. But if he's told it's only once, I think he'll be reasonable." Nkosi took a big breath.

"All right, I'll try, but there are no guarantees."

The following afternoon the Princess entered the throne room carrying a basket of dates, oranges, and clusters of dark red grapes. Pharaoh smiled at his daughter and descended the steps to give her a kiss on her forehead. "Father, I've brought you some fruit and a new invention that my adopted son Moses has made."

"What new invention?"

"He calls it a colander."

Pharaoh looked puzzled. "I have enough calendars. I don't need any more."

"No, Father—not a 'calendar'—a 'colander'. It's a bowl with many holes."

"What good is a defective bowl?"

"You put the grapes in the bowl and run water over them to clean them."

Pharaoh shook his head. "I never cleaned grapes in my life. My cooks do that chore."

"Of course, Father, this will make it easier for your cooks. It's a clever invention."

"If you say so."

The Princess hesitated. "Father, I heard that you wouldn't let my son celebrate his birthday in the palace with his biological family."

"You heard right. No Hebrews can enter this palace."

"He promises to do this only once and no one has to know that they're Hebrews. Please father let him do this once in his life."

"I don't know why I should. I am the powerful ruler of Upper and Lower Egypt and my word is law."

The Princess cast her eyes on the marble floor. "I love you and I hope you love me enough to grant me this wish."

"Okay. I say it's okay just this once."

Nkosi, you see, though he was clay in his wife's hands, he was a diamond to Pharaoh. Unbelievably he turned out unmistakably, to be the best Chief Vizier that Egypt ever had.

Nkosi related Pharaoh's message by quoting him. "I have decided to allow Moses' family to come to my palace, one time and only one time."

Moses leaped up with joy when he heard the good news. Planning a special party for his brother delighted Moses. At that time you couldn't call it a *bar mitzvah,* but it was an event, a wonderful time to celebrate. A dining room sixty cubits from the throne room was set aside for the party. Nowadays boys who become thirteen have parties as large and as elaborate as weddings. They are given gifts. They used to get fountain pens, but we're talking about biblical times and fountain pens hadn't yet been invented.

When Yocheved and Amram and Miriam and Aaron entered the dining room, one musician played the harp and a second one played a flute. The whole family hugged Moses and he embraced them with joy in his heart.

The table was set with a white linen cloth, gold-trimmed dishes of porcelain, and goblets. There were platters of different pieces of fish and all kinds of salads. Bottles of blood of the Nile were at every setting. When they sat down to eat, Amram said a prayer thanking the Lord God for the food and for the health and safety of his family.

Yocheved picked up a pottery bowl. "This is exquisite," she said. "Our pottery is made of red earthenware from Nile mud. It's never decorated, but look at these bowls with geometric forms." She looked at another one. "This one is decorated with flamingoes. It's beautifully polished and white. We poor people drink beer from crudely made goblets of thick clay. We eat our bread from coarse plates while royalty has fine attractive vessels."

Amram looked at his wife with astonishment. "You admire expensive things but you forget that we have a religion that teaches us truth and respect and love for all peoples. The Egyptians have made slaves of us."

"You're right, my husband. But I'm not jealous, just impressed."

Since they had been hungry, they did partake of the various appealing foods and drinks. All of a sudden Yocheved moved her chair away from her salad plate. "Oh my," she cried out.

"What's the matter?" Amram asked.

"There's a big brown bug in my salad."

"Don't let it upset you, my dear. It won't eat much."

"You joke with me. You know I hate bugs."

Amram pushed the plate away. "I'm sorry. You can eat my salad. I'll have more fish."

After the main course servants brought in platters of delicacies, bowls of water, and cloths for the guests to clean and dry their hands. The servants bowed as they left the room.

The family offered a prayer to God after they finished eating.

Then the servants entered to clear the table. Amram noticed that they counted all the expensive plates and goblets. *The Egyptians think we're thieves. How upsetting!*

When the servants left, Moses asked his father a question. "How are our people faring under Pharaoh's harsh decree?"

Amram's face fell. "Everyday life gets harder for us. We're slaving away to build all kinds of temples, pyramids, obelisks, and homes. The brutal taskmasters beat us mercilessly, especially when we don't work fast enough to please them."

"I'm so sorry, *Abba*. I wish I could help," Moses said as tears filled his eyes. Then he wiped his eyes with his hand and said, "I have an idea. Nkosi is my protector. He has horses and chariots in his stable. You're an experienced craftsman. Perhaps he would employ you to fix his chariots?"

"It would be a miracle if you could arrange such a job for me."

Just then Nkosi entered the dining room. The family bowed to him. "Have you enjoyed the food and drink you had?" he asked as he took a seat next to Moses.

"We have," Amram said. "You have been very gracious to us and we thank you for your hospitality."

"I wish to ask a favor," Moses said.

Nkosi nodded.

"My father Amram is an accomplished craftsman. He can be trained as a wheelwright to form rims for your chariot wheels. He knows how to shape a piece of wood with an ad."

Nkosi laughed.

Moses asked, "Why do you laugh, Great Vizier?"

Nkosi smiled as he answered, "The tool is not an 'ad.' It is called an 'adze'. I used to call it an 'ad' myself. I can use another worker. Your father is hired."

"Thank you," Moses said. "You won't be sorry."

"I'll see," Nkosi said. "Amram, report to work tomorrow at sunrise and you'll learn to heat pieces of wood and immerse them in boiling water to soften them until they can be bent to the desired shape. Then you will let them dry."

After Nkosi left, Moses said to his father, "I guess I just got you into hot water."

Amram replied, "That's funny, though it hurts a little. But you have been instrumental in taking me from the cruel hands of the taskmasters and bringing me to an easier job. Your heart is good and noble. I'm so lucky to have you and Aaron and Miriam and your dear mother, who is afraid of bugs. We are the descendants of Abraham, Isaac, and Jacob. Be proud of who you are."

CHAPTER 7

WITH THE EXCEPTION of myself, Methuselah, I wish to fill in some information about Moses that no one knows. The Bible doesn't give a description of his appearance, perhaps because Moses was embarrassed by his countenance. Poor Moses was afflicted with scars on his face. This affected him emotionally. Later on I'll tell you how this emotional distress played itself out.

At the age of fourteen one morning when Moses arose from his bed he felt a funny sensation on his face and found it had broken out with large, solid, painful lumps. He dressed quickly and raced to the court physician. "I have a severe sickness," he said to Dr. Menkhaf. "I think I'm going to die."

The physician took Moses outside in the sun and peered at the bumps. "You aren't going to die for a long, long time. You have what many teenagers get. It's called 'acne.' The pimples will heal slowly. When one begins to go away, others will crop up."

"Is there a cure?" Moses asked, hoping against hope that there was.

"You can try mixing honey and almond oil. You warm up the mixture and apply it as a face mask. But there's no guarantee it will help. Picking at the pimples won't help. Washing with soap and water doesn't cure them. You'll have to learn to live with acne. Eventually you'll have scars on your face that you'll have to live with, as your condition is severe."

"Why do I have acne?"

"You're growing a beard. The openings of hair follicles become clogged with oil secretions and dead skin cells. There is no medication that I know of for this condition."

Moses took this news very hard. He went down to the Nile and dunked his body and his head in the river, hoping that this affliction would disappear. That didn't happen, but he bathed daily in the Nile never giving up hope until one year later he blurted out to Princess Mother, "I'm homely."

"I don't think so," the Princess replied. "To me you are the most handsome teenager in the palace."

"I have pimples, and bumps, and blackheads like you can't imagine. How can you say I'm handsome?"

"I don't see these pimples. I love you, and love sees only beauty."

Moses was enrolled in an archery class with the royal boys. He learned how to shoot a five-foot bow made from a horn. His arms and back ached from the relentless practice but he didn't mind the pain. He stood in a line facing the wall before a row of straw targets. He shot with a natural feel for the spring of the bow and the line of the arrow. Bracing his bow against his stiff right arm, he lined up his target and sent his arrow straight into the middle of it. He became the best of the royal boy archers. This skill helped to increase his self-confidence that had slipped because of his acne.

Hatshepsut, the royal princess, approached her father as he sat on his throne eating a pickle. "My adopted son Moses is now fifteen-years-old and pining to visit his older brother. He has asked me to get your permission to let him go to Goshen for a short visit."

"You know that the Hebrews are my enemies. He may be a spy. I can't grant this request," Pharaoh said as he took a huge sip of water.

"Please Father, Moses is trustworthy. He's not a spy. He'll visit for just a few hours. I'll bring you more pickles from my stock."

"How many pickles?" Pharaoh asked, as his eyes opened wide with anticipation.

"Two dozen juicy pickles that my cook prepared from cucumbers."

"All right. He can go, but only tomorrow from sunrise until the ball of the sun is directly overhead."

Moses and Aaron took a stroll near the river Nile. "How is your life in the palace?" Aaron asked.

Moses looked sad. "I've no time for recreation."

"What's keeping you so busy?"

"I sit in a classroom in the palace learning history, geography, mathematics, writing, literature, philosophy, and Egyptian law. I also have to study *The Book of the Dead*."

"Wow," Aaron said. "Did the dead write a book?"

"Don't joke around. That's not really funny. I feel like I have no time for myself. I don't eat lunch. Egyptians don't snack. I also take boxing lessons and painting lessons. But I do have a secret."

Aaron looked interested. "You can tell me your secret. I promise I won't reveal it."

"All right. In the middle of the night, when everyone is fast asleep, I climb up to the roof. I have studied how a palm tree is shaped and I've taken wooden poles and linen cloth and I designed what I call a "brella." The top is shaped like a triangle. I put a pole in the center that I hold onto. Then I jump off the roof and sail to the ground without getting hurt. I fly like a bird. It lifts my mood and makes me happy."

Aaron clapped his hands. "I always knew you were brilliant. I'd like to try the same thing."

Moses shook his head. "You need the exact measurements. It's fun, but I would be afraid you'll get injured and I'd get the blame."

Aaron placed his hand on his brother's shoulder. "An Egyptian may catch you doing that one night and your secret would be revealed. I advise you to stop doing your 'brella thing'."

"You're right. I get very tired in class and I need a better night's sleep. I'll just try out my "brella" once more and then I'll stop."

I, Methuselah, am aware that Leonardo da Vinci imagined and sketched the first modern conical parachute. But I know for sure that it was Moses who preceded him in inventing the parachute and he should be given credit for this significant accomplishment.

When Moses was almost sixteen, he was placed in a special class to help him with his speech impediment. The class was composed of five students from the ages of thirteen to sixteen. There was a sixteen-year-old student by the name of Anubis, who was named after the jackal god. He was coarse, calculating, and selfish. Anubis was a troublesome young man prone to cause dissension, and even disruption, in the class. He was a stutterer, and that is what may have caused him to act out.

On the other hand, a shy and sensitive sixteen-year-old girl sat next to Anubis. Her name was Nenet, and she was named after the goddess of the deep. She mispronounced some letters in Egyptian. She wasn't afflicted by acne. In fact, her skin was the color of alabaster. However, her speech sensitivity was responsible for an overeating habit and she became rather plump.

Anubis used to tease Nenet cruelly. As soon as she came into class and before the teacher entered, Anubis sat down and said to her things like, "You look like the biggest cow in my father's herd."

After hearing this kind of insult Nenet used to put her hands over her eyes and weep. Moses warned Anubis to stop this bullying, but Anubis didn't listen. He shouted louder, "Nanet is a fat slob. Nanet is a fat fat slob. Nanet is a fat fat fat slob."

A fountain of tears used to roll down Nenet's face. Moses felt sorry for the girl and once when he lost his temper, just as the teacher entered the classroom, he punched Anubis in his jaw loosening two of his teeth.

Moses was sent to his chamber by way of punishment. Nkosi came to him. "I heard how you hit Anubis. You were right to upbraid him, but you should watch your temper and not flare up. This could get you into hot water someday."

"He deserved what I did to him," Moses said.

"I'm sure he did," Nkosi said, "but you should have let the teacher handle him. It's all right to be angry, but it's not all right for you to take matters into your own hands. Do you like Nenet? Are you attracted to her? Do you think she's pretty? I wouldn't be surprised if you were. She's a knockout."

"Yes, I like her a lot. She's a lovely girl and very shy. But she is Egyptian and I have to reserve my heart for Hebrew girls."

"I understand. I wonder if we were wrong to have given you boxing lessons." Nkosi wrinkled his forehead. "You have learned fighting too well."

"I needed those boxing lessons. I may have to defend myself sometime in the future. But I will try hard not to lose my temper."

"That's good. I don't want to see you get into trouble. The Princess loves you very much and she wants you to be safe."

"I love her, too. She's been unbelievably good to me and I don't want to cause her aggravation."

"I have an idea," Nkosi said. "Next year when you're sixteen I'll enroll you in an independent unit in Pharaoh's military force. You'll be trained to drive a chariot. How are you doing in Egyptian religious learning?"

"I get all A's. I've memorized *The Book of the Dead*."

Moses felt guilty about studying and practicing Egyptian religion. *I'm living a double life. Outwardly I dress like Egyptian royalty. I pray to their gods in public. My friends are Egyptians and they have no idea who I really am. I have to come up with a way to keep secret my belief in one God and lie at the same time.* Moses thought a lot about his subterfuge, the lying at every turn which he was forced to do. As a result he became the first person who crossed his middle and index fingers when he told an untruth. We should be grateful to Moses not only for what he accomplished later in his life, but also for this innovative technique.

Another accomplishment of Moses was that he invented the game of golf. One spring day Moses was in the palace garden picking some oranges off a tree in an orchard. He ate two oranges and kicked away the third one with his sandal. In reality he should've disposed of it in the trash can inside the palace. But Moses was in a playful mood. The air was fresh and warmed by the bright sun. *I would love to stay outdoors and skip my lesson on architecture.* After a few minutes Moses decided to kick another orange to see how far he could send it. He plucked one from the bottom branch of the tree. He sent the orange flying but couldn't see where it landed. He shaded his eyes with his hand but the orange had disappeared. *Where is it?* Moses walked twenty paces on the grass and discovered a gopher hole. The orange had dropped into the hole. He was delighted. He picked up the orange and came up with the idea that he would break off the bottom branch and try to hit another orange into the hole. He had learned from his mother that eighteen was a lucky Hebrew number and that was how that night when Moses was in bed he developed the idea of people hitting balls into eighteen holes. And that's how the game of golf originated.

The next morning Moses approached Nkosi with his novel idea. Nkosi tilted his head and fell deep in thought. He grinned from one end of his mouth to another. "Moses, that's a great idea. I'll speak to Pharaoh about it." Soon afterwards Pharaoh directed the architects to construct fairways and putting greens. When the project had been completed, Nkosi asked Moses, "How will people find out about our golf course?"

"I'll put an ad in the *Egyptian Times* describing it. What should I call the golf course?"

Nkosi came right out with the name. "Call it 'Moses' Golf Course,' of course."

All the members of royalty flocked together to enjoy the ingenious game. The nobility did as well and they all became beholden to Moses for this wonderful innovation.

Chariot drivers formed an elite force in the military. They delivered the first strike. They were much faster than foot-soldiers. The light chariots contained one warrior armed with bow and spear and one driver. Moses began to be trained as a warrior when he reached the age of sixteen. He plied the bow with accuracy even when the horse was at a full gallop. What he liked was not the battle but the white horse that pulled his chariot. It was a large horse, broad of girth, which had a long white mane that waved in the air as the horse pranced and reared. Moses gave him treats with lumps of sugar and baby carrots. He named his horse Abraham. He painted his chariot with pictures of date palms. Though Moses had become a very capable artist, he was never given credit for this in the Bible.

Since Moses was a peaceful person, he had compunctions about using the bow and spear which were designed to kill Egypt's enemies. He approached Nkosi outside the stable, "My horse is swift and I'd like to drive the chariot instead of being a warrior. Furthermore, I'm a good driver and can hold the whip and the reins easily since my hands are strong."

Nkosi shaded his eyes from the radiant desert sun which beat down through the cloudless blue sky. "I don't know about that. You are a marvelous archer—much better than many."

"Please, Great Vizier, I have a deep feeling against killing people, even if they are our enemies."

Nkosi tapped his temple with his broad fingers. "I give my permission for you to be a driver."

"Thank you. I'll try to be the best chariot driver in your army," Moses said with his hesitant speech.

What Moses did to improve the speed of the chariot was to make it lighter. He changed the position of the chariot's axle, making it closer to the driver. He was also responsible for covering parts of the axle with metal, which reduced the friction between the axle and the wheelhub. He replaced heavy wood chariot parts by lighter ones with metal sleeves. The lighter chariots were both more efficient and easier for the horses to pull.

One morning after his speech class he approached Nkosi. "Great Vizier, I have an idea that since Egypt doesn't have the proper wood for our chariots we should import wood."

"What kind of wood?" Nkosi asked.

"We should import ash and elm to strengthen the axles. For the footboard we need to import sycamore."

"I will look into this," Nkosi said. "Right now we aren't at war with Ethiopia to the south, so it's possible to import these woods from that country."

This plan was put into effect and Moses received recognition by Pharaoh with gifts of gold jewelry, a large statue of the god Osiris, and a medal of commendation.

When Moses was seventeen, Egypt was at peace. He realized that the Egyptians were growing restless. They needed a new form of entertainment. In biblical times there were no movies, casinos, radios, or television. Moses was the first one to come up with the idea of establishing chariot races. He approached Nkosi with the proposition.

Nkosi liked the idea and went to the throne room to discuss the feasibility of his idea. He was surprised to see Mrs. Pharaoh in the throne next to her husband. Her dark eyes were contoured with kohl which accidently had rubbed down her cheek. Nkosi bowed and addressed Pharaoh, "My Lord Goodness Gracious, Moses, has recommended for your consideration building a race track to hold chariot races for the amusement of the populace."

Pharaoh frowned. "I'm not interested in spending money for the entertainment of my subjects. I veto the idea."

Mrs. Pharaoh held up her hand. "Just one minute, my Lord, before you dismiss this idea."

"Yes, dear," Pharaoh said. Have I told you that Mrs. Pharaoh constantly hen-pecked her husband. I, as Methuselah, know this for a fact. Many times she contradicted and even overruled her husband.

Mrs. Pharaoh continued, "There are advantages to having chariot races. For instance, we would need a grandstand for people to watch the races. The grandstand and the track could be erected by our Hebrew slaves. They don't have enough work as it is. You could have your artisans design a trophy with your picture on it for the winner of the race. Our subjects would appreciate that you have taken their entertainment needs seriously. You can name the site 'Egypt Downs.' Also, when visiting dignitaries will be present, they'll be happy and impressed to enjoy such an event. Chariot racing will be recognized as the 'Sport of Kings,' and you will be honored as the first ruler to have introduced it. Our scribes will note this on papyrus and stone monuments. Other less advanced nations will follow your example. Don't you agree that I'm making sense?"

"Yes, dear."

When Nkosi told Moses the good news, Moses was delighted. He practiced four hours a day with his horse. He fed the three-year-old Arabian stallion healthful greens that were cultivated by his mother. He did sprinting exercises with his horse, and he rubbed him down for a half hour after every workout.

Hebrew slaves were brought in to build a level dirt track since the chariots were very expensive and prone to breakdowns on uneven terrain. They hurt their backs clearing the land of rocks. Pharaoh's architects designed the track to be a straight path. Other Hebrews worked building the grandstand and keeping the chariots in tip-top shape.

Over a hundred teen-aged boys applied for the race. Moses narrowed the number of entries down to four drivers and their chariots. A committee of three royal subjects selected Moses, Anubis, Bunson, and Clayton. Moses, arguably the best driver in all of Egypt, couldn't be excluded, although inevitable complaints about nepotism were raised.

It was a cloudless sunny day for the first chariot race in history. An announcer with a booming voice described everything from beginning to end. "This is a four-race competition. The participants are entering the track riding chariots that are pulled by Arabian horses. First we have Prince Moses, seventeen, the son of the Princess. His horse is the mighty stallion Abraham. Next is Anubis, eighteen. His horse is Jawa. Next to him is Bunson, fifteen, with Riyadh, a filly. Clayton, seventeen, has Badr as his horse.

"The chariots are lining up one by one at the barrier. The horses are snorting. Excitement is in the air. The ram's horn just signaled the start of the race. They're off. They're running like the wind. There they go. Moses is in the post position. Anubis is next to Malik. Taking the lead is Anubis. Second is Moses, whose horse is at a full gallop. Third is Bunson. Coming up fast from the rear is Clayton.

"Now Moses is leading. He's running like a cyclone. Anubis is lashing his horse with a whip. Anubis is in the lead, Moses is second, Clayton now is third, and Bunson is in the rear. Anubis and Moses are neck and neck. Now Anubis is leading. Moses and Anubis are nose to nose.

"Uh, oh, Anubis is very close to Moses' chariot. Anubis just hurled a spike at Moses' chariot. Moses' chariot with the cross-bar spokes is tottering from side to side. Anubis is leading with Moses close behind. The crowd is shouting something, but I can't make it out. Anubis wins the race. Moses is second. Bunson comes in third.

"Just a minute folks. There's an announcement from the judges. Anubis has been declared out of the running for making an illegal move. Moses displayed excellent horsemanship. He's jumping out of his chariot. He's walking toward the stands. The applause is deafening. Moses is accepting the trophy that Pharaoh is handing him. He's bowing and holding up the trophy with Pharaoh's picture on it. The crowd is going wild with cheers and applause. Moses is bowing to the crowd.

"Now Moses with a fierce look is approaching Anubis. He's pulling Anubis from his chariot. Moses is taking a boxing stance. He's landing a powerful right fist squarely against Anubis' chin. Then, a second and a third blow.

He's repeatedly connecting his fist flush with Anubis' chin. Anubis is collapsing on the ground from the beating. Blood is spurting from his mouth. He just spit out one tooth, no—correction—two teeth. The Medical Emergency Guards are racing to his side. They're carrying him away to the hospital for treatment. Moses is rubbing his right hand which seems to be injured. The crowd is on its feet screaming, 'Hurray for Moses! Hurray for Moses!' This has been a day that will go down in history. This is your announcer signing off."

One man in the stands exclaimed to his friend, "I won. I put two gold coins on Moses and he came in first. How did you do?"

"I put silver coins on win, place, and show and I won the trifecta. Let's go collect."

"All right. Don't you think it will be better from now on to gamble on chariot races than on golf?"

"You bet. I hope they have these races every week. We'll clean up."

I, Methuselah, am acquainted with the evolution of gambling and Moses was instrumental in its growth also. In the twentieth century an actor by the name of Eddie Cantor applauded Moses with this ditty:

> "If you knew Susie like I know Susie
> Oh, oh what a girl
> There's no one so classy
> As this fair lassie
> Oh, oh, *Holy Moses,*
> What a chassis."

CHAPTER 8

NKOSI ENTERED MOSES'S chamber and watched as Moses put his injured hand in a bowl filled to the brim with cold water. "I want to congratulate you, but I see we can't shake hands," Nkosi said. He noticed the pain on Moses' face. "Did you break any bones?"

"No, I'm okay. Did you see how Anubis threw the rod into my wheel?"

"Yes, I saw it. It was a terrible thing for him to do. But you shouldn't have punched him. You broke his jaw. He lost some of his front teeth."

"He needed to learn a lesson." Moses took his hand out of the bowl with the cold water. He rubbed his hand to ease the pain. "I'm sorry. I didn't mean to do that. I just. . . ." Moses managed a feeble smile.

"This is a serious offense," Nkosi said. "I predict that your temper will get you in trouble in the future, and I've warned you about that in the past. You have to learn how to deal with anger. I have conceived of a new way to help people control their anger and I have instituted what I call an 'Anger Management' class. This class will teach you tips on how to control your temper."

"I'm royalty of the house of Pharaoh. I won't attend. I'll monitor my own temper in the future, thank you."

Nkosi sighed. "You have no choice. Pharaoh has ordered you to sign up for this class. Anubis is enrolled also."

Moses shook his head and swallowed his saliva.

The classroom that Moses stepped into was small. Five chairs were placed around a table. The teacher, an older Egyptian by the name of Professor Abraxas, sat in one chair. He had a nose like a hawk and thin lips. Moses bowed to him and took a seat next to Aaheru, whose name meant "The Chief of Terrors." Aaheru was twenty, so big and brawny that he reminded Moses of his horse Abraham. Next to Aaheru was Aaani, whose name meant "Ape." Moses thought that that name was appropriate in view of Aaani's thick black hair on his chest, arms, and legs.

When Anubis came in and looked around, he spotted Moses. Quick as a ferret he struck Moses and Moses retaliated by punching Anubis in his belly. Aaheru jumped up and separated them. He sat between Moses and his nemesis Anubis.

Professor Abraxas began to talk in a pompous bombastic way. He sermonized how injurious it is to display aggressive anger that quickly turns to rage. He said, "It's vulgar and foolish, and it results in serious, brutal, and bloody outcomes." As he became more and more loquacious, his voice became strident. Moses wished he could stuff his ears with cotton.

"Take out your papyrus and start taking notes," the professor said. "Write 'UNCONTROLLED ANGER CAN TAKE A TOLL ON MY HEALTH. I CAN GET HIGH BLOOD PRESSURE. I CAN BE INJURED OR LOSE

MY LIFE. I CAN DAMAGE MY RELATIONSHIPS'. Stop writing!"

After ten minutes when the students were finished, the professor said, "Aaani, why are you still writing?"

Aaani looked crestfallen. "I don't know how to write 'relationships' in hieroglyphs."

"I'll show you," Moses said.

The professor waited a minute before asking, "Is there any student here who is married?"

Aaheru held up his beefy hand.

Professor Abraxas said, "Do you lose your temper with your wife?"

Aaheru nodded in the affirmative. His face reflected sadness.

"Speak up," the professor said.

"Yes, sometimes when she's late with dinner, I yell at her. I never hit her."

Professor Abraxas said, "Someday your wife may leave you for another man who is more soft-spoken than you. Students, start writing again. 'THINK BEFORE YOU SPEAK.' You may regret what you say in the heat of the moment, so when you feel you are about to lose your temper take a few moments to collect your thoughts. Anger is a normal and healthy emotion, but you have to deal with it in a positive way. For example, when I saw Moses and Anubis fighting, I got angry, but I said nothing and the situation calmed down."

Moses thought, *What an idiot. He didn't notice that Aaheru had separated us. I would've clobbered Anubis if he hadn't.*

Aaheru raised his hand.

"What is it?" the teacher asked.

"May I be excused?"

"No, you have to wait."

"I can't!"

"Then make it snappy. I'll wait until you get back. The tips I'm giving you are not only important for your relationships, but vital to your health and general well-being."

"Yes, Professor, I'll come back as soon as I can."

After five minutes had passed the professor said, "Class dismissed!" even though Aaheru had not yet returned.

Moses and Anubis avoided each other as they left the classroom.

Yocheved was seated at her kitchen table finishing a cheese sandwich on rye when Moses stamped into the house with a livid expression on his face. He sat down opposite her. "I'm going berserk," he complained to his mother.

She swallowed the last bite. "What's wrong?"

"I'm in a despicable, odious, backward class that the high-and-mighty Pharaoh has commanded me to take."

"Shush," Yocheved said, as she put her index finger to her mouth. "You're talking treason. You're putting yourself and our family in danger. "What kind of class are you talking about?"

"Anubis, my nemesis, tossed a rod into the wheel of my chariot. I would've lost the race if what he did hadn't been declared illegal. I got angry and hit him."

Yocheved nodded. "I understand your frustration, but you should've just expressed how angry you were and gotten over it."

"That's what Nkosi told me. I was placed in an Anger Management class and I hate it."

"My dear son, it seems to me you don't have a choice. I advise you to make the best of the situation and learn what you can about how to deal with your anger. It could be that someday in the future that knowledge will come in handy."

The next day Professor Abraxas announced, "If any of you students have a reason to leave during the lesson, you aren't free to go. You should have taken care of what you needed to do before class began."

All the students sat erect like toy soldiers. Moses and Anubis glared at each other. Anubis couldn't talk because of his injured jaw, but if looks could kill, the look he shot at Moses would have buried Moses alive.

Professor Abraxas said, "Start writing this important tip on your papyrus, 'TRY TO EXPRESS WHY YOU ARE ANGRY IN A CALM WAY.'"

Aaani raised his hand.

"What is it?"

"I don't know how to write 'calm.'"

Moses said, "I'll show you."

The professor continued with a touch of annoyance in his voice, "Assert yourself in a nonconfrontational way. Say why you're angry clearly and directly without hurting anyone or trying to control them."

Aaheru raised his hand.

Professor Abraxas looked angry. "What is it?"

Aaheru said, "When I'm angry, I can't talk."

The professor said, "Force yourself to change."

"I'll try, but I can't guarantee results."

"If you don't change," the professor said, ". . . you'll have to keep repeating this class until you do."

"Yes, sir."

"Now write down the next suggestion, 'GET EXERCISE.' You, Aaani, the hieroglyph for 'exercise' is a running figure. The next tip is 'RELAXATION.' The hieroglyph for that is a figure in a bed. You need to practice deep-breathing exercises. I want the four of you to stand and take deep breaths. Now sit down and say 'Take it easy' fifteen times. Anubis, you can't talk so you are excused, except repeat 'Take it easy' in your mind. There will be a test tomorrow about what I expect you have already learned. Class dismissed."

After class Aaani approached Moses. "I think we should relax this afternoon before we take the test."

"What do you have in mind?"

"I have a girlfriend and she has a girlfriend. Why don't we have a picnic in two hours? We can relax sitting on the bank of the river Nile."

"I think that's a good idea. I never went on a picnic. I'll bring the food. You bring the drinks."

Aaani showed up with two young women. He introduced his girl as Lapis and the other girl as Lateefah. Moses felt comfortable with Lateefah because she also had pimples on her face. *When her acne disappears, she'll be a beauty*, Moses thought.

They sat down on the river bank. Moses gave each person fruits, cheese, and bread.

Lateefah said, "Thank you."

"My pleasure," Moses said. "I know that your name means 'pleasant and kind' and I see you're pleasant and courteous, as your name indicates."

When they finished eating and drinking, Aaani took Lapis' hand and they went for a walk leaving Moses and Lateefah alone.

Moses' face reddened. *I'm attracted to this girl, but I know that when I marry it can't be to an Egyptian. I would like to date her but I better not.*

The following day the professor said, "This is a written test. If I find you cheating by copying from your neighbor's papyrus, I'll report you to Pharaoh for punishment. Keep your eyes on your own papyrus. When you finish the test, you're free to go."

The next day the professor said with a straight face, "I'm satisfied to report that all of you passed the test with a perfect score. The following tip is about the role of humor in diffusing anger. Write this down, 'USE HUMOR TO RELEASE TENSION.' I will give you an example of humor. You may tell this joke to a person who is making you angry.

"A rich father gives his son two camels for his birthday. The son is excited and says, 'Thank you for the wonderful gifts.' He mounts one camel in an attempt to ride it. The father says, 'What's the matter? You don't like the other one!'"

All the students laugh quietly with the exception of Anubis with the injured jaw.

The professor next tried another joke. "An Egyptian wife makes a party for her friends. As they get ready to leave, one woman says, 'I loved your date-and-nut cookies. They were so delicious I ate four of them.'

'You ate five,' the hostess says, 'but who's counting?'"

This time the students were more enthusiastic. All of them smiled and clapped their hands.

The professor offered a weak smile in response. "The next tip," he said, ". . . is very important. Write this. No, don't write this tip because there is no hieroglyph for 'TIMEOUT.' You need to give yourself short breaks when you find yourself under stress. Quiet time may help you feel better prepared without your getting angry in order to be able to handle situations that provoke you."

Moses raised his hand.

"What is it?" the professor asked with a frown.

"I have boxing lessons in the morning, followed by chariot exercises, followed by religious teachings, followed by a class in architecture, followed by my art class. Then I have lunch for fifteen minutes. After lunch I have speech and medical lessons. Then I go to your Anger Management class. I have no time for the 'TIMEOUT' you just mentioned. What should I do?"

"Umm," the professor said. "You may skip TIMEOUT by taking extra breaths. Now, class, I will give you the next to the last tip for dealing with anger. Write this down 'MAKE "I" STATEMENTS.' This means that instead of placing blame and increasing tension, use 'I' statements to describe the problem. Be specific and respectful. For example, when Moses got upset at Anubis he could've said, 'I'm upset that you damaged my chariot' instead of pummeling him."

Moses raised his hand.

"What is it?"

"That would've been impossible at the time. My anger boiled over. What he did was unforgivable."

Anubis got up from his chair and faced Moses with a closed fist, ready to punch him. Aaheru stopped him. Anubis's face turned crimson as he sat back down.

Professor Abraxas held up his hand. "I've been delaying this last tip because it's the best. Students, write 'DON'T HOLD A GRUDGE.' The hieroglyphs are two figures. The first figure has a scowl on his face; the second figure is smiling. Forgiveness is powerful. If you can forgive a person who angered you, you might learn from the situation. Both of you may actually strengthen your relationship. Now that you have this tip, I want Moses and Anubis to forgive each other and shake hands."

Moses arose, left his seat, glared with anger at Anubis, and walked towards the door. He declared, "Not a chance. I'm glad this class has ended. Sorry, Professor, but I haven't learned anything. I can't take time out from my busy schedule. I don't tell jokes, and I don't consider many things to be funny at all."

CHAPTER 9

IT WAS NOON the following day and Moses was sitting in the student's lunchroom when Nkosi marched in. He sat opposite Moses who was eating a bagel with lox and cream cheese. With a sad expression he said, "What I'm going to tell you won't make you laugh. You may even cry."

Moses opened his eyes wide. "What is it?"

"Professor Abraxas went to the throne room and told Pharaoh what you had said when you left the classroom. Mrs. Pharaoh was there. She advised her husband to order you to repeat the class. He agreed. He always agrees with her. As a consequence, you have been left back."

Moses threw the rest of his bagel sandwich at the wall. Students who were seated near him looked shocked at this uncouth breach of decorum. "I'll leave the palace before I go back to that idiotic class."

"You'll be making a big mistake," Nkosi said. "Your royal education isn't complete. You're still a teenager and have a lot to learn. I advise you to go to the next class. Anubis won't be there. Three other youths, one male and two females, have been selected as students for the next Anger Management class. You don't have to contribute anything. Just sit and listen and pretend that you are comfortable in the class."

"I would be living a lie," Moses said.

"What would your parents say if you dropped out? Perhaps Pharaoh would order you out of the palace. If you left, how could you help your family and fellow Hebrews?"

Moses put his chin in his hands. "You're right. If I were banished in disgrace, I wouldn't be able to help my family and my people." He sighed, "Okay, you're right. I'll go back, but I won't like it."

"That's a wise decision. Nobody says you have to like it. You can lump it, as they say. I'm proud of you. Someday you'll be an important figure. People will remember you, Moses, for generations to come."

The next Anger Management class started the following week. Moses took his seat next to a sixteen-year-old boy who introduced himself. "My name is Tacitus. I was a quiet baby so my parents gave me that name, which means 'quiet.' They had a thing for Latin names. Believe me, I'm not quiet anymore. I yell like a cow giving birth to a calf and I hit people I don't like."

"I'm glad to meet you, Tacitus. I'm Moses and my name means 'drawn from the water.'"

The door opened and two attractive fifteen-year-old females bounded in. One was shorter than an average Egyptian girl, and the other one was as tall as Moses, who was six-feet. When they saw how handsome and muscular Moses was, each one fought to sit next to him. They kept slapping each other until the professor arrived and demanded that they sit down.

Professor Abaxis asked each one to state his or her name and give the reason that they were here.

"My name is Moses. I lose my temper and sometimes punch a person I believe is unfair."

"My name is Tacitus and I'm sorry to say that I hit my dogs when they bark too much."

The short girl, who had managed to sit next to Moses, said, "I'm Tadita which means 'the running one,' and I don't like Panni because she teases me about my height, so I slap her."

"My name is Panni, which means 'gracious,' and if Tadita wouldn't make fun of how tall I am, I wouldn't fight with her. I don't like her, though, because she's as small as a skunk."

Professor Abraxas said with a sharp expression, "You are here to learn how to get along with one another. The first rule is that we don't insult people. We say, 'My feelings are hurt when you tease me.'"

Tacitus raised his hand and when the professor nodded, he asked, "Do we need to bring supplies?"

"Yes, next time make sure you bring a quill and ink and a roll of papyrus so you can write down all the rules for peacemaking. Moses didn't take this Anger Management class seriously and he will be repeating the class until he learns to conform."

Moses looked out the window at the swaying palm trees. *This teacher is a fool. No rules can help me when I lose my temper, but I have to keep my thoughts to myself or I'll be taking this class over and over again until I'm an old man.*

The Hebrew slaves were in a weakened condition and unable to work as hard as before. Mrs. Pharaoh was miffed and she brought this to the attention of her husband when they were seated in the throne room. "Rammy, you need to punish the slaves who are shirking their duty. I heard that there are some who take coffee breaks when they should be working at building an obelisk."

"Yes, Dear Heart. What do you propose I should do?"

At the very same moment when Mrs. Pharaoh pointed her bony finger at her husband, Moses entered the throne room to report that Anubis was teasing Tadita by sending her insulting notes. He stood quietly behind the life-sized statue of Osiris, one of the Egyptian gods, unnoticed by both majesties. He listened with interest as Mrs. Pharaoh spoke. "I want you to appoint Anubis as Chief Taskmaster. He's as tough as they come. Anubis will deal harshly with the slaves who are goofing off. The slaves will be so frightened that they'll work harder."

"Yes, Honey Date."

Moses backed away without being observed. He went looking for Nkosi to report the disturbing news and found him in the employees' dining room eating some olives. "Anubis has been a thorn in my side," Moses complained to Nkosi, his mentor and friend.

"Have you fought with him again?" Nkosi asked.

"No, but I've learned that since he's of royalty he is to be appointed Chief Taskmaster. I know he'll be cruel to my people—as if they haven't suffered enough."

"There's nothing you can do about that, Moses."

"When he's officially appointed, I can follow him and see what he does."

Nkosi took a bite of a pickle. "I don't think that's a good idea. It could get you into trouble."

"I don't care. I have to protect my people."

Moses was in the royal students' dining room when he overheard the boys Bek and Hapu whispering. He hated gossip but this was too juicy an item to disregard. Bek leaned over to hear what Hapu had to say. "Aaheru, the student who is built like an elephant, was in the Anger Management class. I heard him say to Moses that sometimes he feels like killing his wife."

"Did he say how?" Bek asked with raised brows.

"He said that he would throw a rock at her head."

Moses choked on a slice of the apple he had been eating when he heard such nonsense. It was a total lie. Aaheru had been in his Anger Management class, but Aaheru loved his wife and hadn't told him he had thoughts of murdering her. Meanwhile the two students left their seats. Moses coughed and swallowed a glass of water to clear his throat. Then he went searching for them to set them straight, but he couldn't locate them.

The following day all the royals in the palace, including Pharaoh and Mrs. Pharaoh, were gossiping about Aaheru who was arrested for the murder of his wife Iput whose head had been bloodied and bruised. Pharaoh said, "Aaheru wasn't placed in the Anger Management class for nothing. He's built like a gorilla and has a fierce temper. I'm not surprised he murdered Iput. I'll have him hanged."

When Moses heard this, he bit down on his lips. *Aaheru has a temper but I don't believe he's capable of murder. He stopped me from hitting Anubis. I will investigate this and see if I can clear him. I don't believe he should be hanged.*

Moses visited Aaheru in the dark and musty jail. Rats were scurrying around. Moses asked Aaheru what happened. "I don't know who killed Iput but it wasn't me."

"Why would anyone kill your wife?" Moses asked.

"She was unfaithful to me," Aaheru said. "Maybe her lover killed her. She was angry at me. I was certainly as angry at her as she had been at me, but it was because she committed adultery."

Moses looked puzzled. "That doesn't look good for you. It provides a motivation for killing her."

"But I didn't," Aaheru protested. "Believe me, Moses, I'm innocent."

"I'll look into this thoroughly," Moses said. "Do you have the key to your chamber?"

Aaheru took it out of the pocket in his robe and handed it to Moses.

That evening Moses opened Aaheru's chamber door. He searched the entire place and found a papyrus of her diary under a cushion. He read her hieroglyphs. "I am very sad about my failing marriage. Aaheru and I no longer speak to each other. I make Aaheru's meals and he doesn't thank me anymore. He looks angry and goes to sleep in another chamber. I don't know what our future will be. Who can predict what a man with an out-of-control temper will do? I suspect that my husband may kill me. If I die, my head will be bruised and bloody. He may not even have me embalmed. I never would have married him if I knew how mean a person he really is."

Moses thought long and hard about the meaning of Iput's words. He deduced that she was so angry with Aaheru that she wanted him to be hanged. She had written about her head being bruised. How would she know that? She didn't realize that her diary would incriminate her. She had committed suicide and made it look like Aaheru had done it.

Moses went to the throne room when Mrs. Pharaoh wasn't there as he realized that she might contradict what he had to reveal. Pharaoh was in a bad mood as one of his obelisks had fallen to the ground.

"What do you want? Pharaoh asked in an angry voice. "Have you invented anything else recently? Your inventions have been costing me a fortune."

"No, Your Royal Highness. I've come to tell you that Aaheru is innocent of killing his wife."

"Innocent? You think he's innocent? So who did kill her?"

Moses took a deep breath. "Sh-sh-she killed herself."

"You mean she committed suicide. It's forbidden for any of my people to commit suicide."

"I know," Moses said. "But she did it to take revenge on Aaheru for finding out about her adultery. She was afraid of being stoned."

"How do you know this?" Pharaoh asked as he fisted his hands.

"I read her diary. She wrote that after her death her head would be bruised and bloody. If she hadn't done this to herself, how could she have predicted it?"

"I want to read her diary for myself," Pharaoh said reaching out for the papyrus Moses had in his hand.

It took Pharaoh a while to decipher Iput's hieroglyphics. He released Aaheru from jail. Moses thus became the first detective in history.

#

One time Moses sat on a stool in the corner of the mummification chamber watching with intense concentration and great interest three doctors mummify a royal prince. He knew how much Egyptians treasured life, and that they believed that after death life continues as it had been before. It was important for them to preserve the body and send it with items that the person treasured to the next world.

Afterwards Moses visited his mother and told her what he had seen. Yocheved said, "We also believe in the next world and that the soul lives on. We bury our dead in the ground almost immediately, but that doesn't mean you shouldn't have respect for the religion of the Egyptians."

"I felt nausea watching this process. Let me tell you about it."

"If that will make you feel better, go ahead," Yocheved said as she patted her son on his arm with her hand.

"First one doctor stuck a hook up the boy's nose and pulled out his brain through his nostrils."

Yocheved gritted her teeth. "It was good he was dead and felt no pain."

"Then another doctor cut the left side of his body and took out his lungs, stomach, liver, and intestines. I was thinking about being a doctor, but when I saw this gory scene I changed my mind."

"What did they do with the icky stuff that came out?" Yocheved asked as she became pale.

"They took everything and put it in separate canopic jars. But then I learned something very interesting. They filled the empty space in the body with bags of natron and sweet-smelling spices."

"What's natron?"

"It's soda ash that preserves the body. The doctors put the body on a slanted table with a jar at the bottom so that the extracted water could be collected. By this time I had it up to here." Moses pointed to the top of his head. "They leave the body to dry out for forty days, and then they clean it with oils and wrap it with linen strips. The entire embalming process takes seventy days."

"Very interesting," Yocheved said with a frown. "I could've lived without knowing about that whole disgusting process. I was going to eat dinner, but now I've lost my appetite."

"Sorry *Imma*, I did learn something useful. Natron dries flesh. It could be used as a preservative for fish. I think I'll try it."

I, Methuselah, say, "Moses was the first one to dry salmon with natron and make lox. The Hebrews should be grateful to him for this tasty invention."

CHAPTER 10

IT BOTHERED MOSES that his nemesis Anubis had become the Chief Taskmaster. He decided to follow him and see how he would act in his new role. Moses disguised himself by wearing a long black robe and a hat that concealed his head. He was practiced in surveillance and wasn't detected. Anubis, with a whip in his hand, quickstepped to his destination. He came upon an exhausted Hebrew slave who sat resting on a boulder, his head in his shriveled hands. Moses recognized the slave as Meyer, the very same man who had taught him how to ride a camel when he had been a child.

Anubis took his whip and, slashing the back of the slave, drew blood. Moses looked around to see if there was an official nearby to administer justice, but there wasn't. He would have to take matters into his own hands.

Anubis raised his whip and was ready to strike again when Moses grabbed the whip and sent it flying. A red flame of anger burned in his heart. He punched Anubis in his stomach. Anubis lost his balance, and fell back on the bolder that the slave had been sitting on. He hit his head and split it open. When Anubis's brain tumbled out, Moses felt his legs quiver like strawberry jelly.

Moses hadn't meant to kill him because he knew that the One God forbade killing. But once more his temper reared up. Moses didn't see any witnesses with the exception of

Meyer. He found the shovel that Meyer had been using. It was made of a scapula from the shoulder blade of an ox. The shovel wasn't strong like those in modern times so it took him an hour to bury Anubis in the sand. Then he raced back to the palace, noticed that his sandals and clothes were sandy, and decided that the first thing he needed to do was take a shower. After he dried off, he changed his clothes before anyone learned what he had done.

The next day when he went back to see how Meyer was faring two Hebrew men were fighting. Moses said to them, "Why are you fighting?"

One said, "Who made you a prince and a judge over us? We know what you did yesterday. Will you kill us like you killed the Egyptian?"

"It was an accident," Moses said. "Even though he was an evil man, I didn't mean to kill him."

"There is no such thing as an accident," the first man said. "You will be punished for what you did. We saw you punch the Egyptian, and we will report this to Pharaoh." They didn't have to do this. I, Methuselah, am angry that they were going to rat on Moses, but it's possible they didn't know that he was a Hebrew like them. Anyway, this turned out to be a good thing as Moses had enjoyed the palace so much he might never have left and the world wouldn't have gotten the Ten Commandments, let alone the Five Books in his name.

Moses' face turned white. His knees began to quiver. He was so frightened he couldn't talk. Right then and there he knew he couldn't return to the palace. He was dressed as an Egyptian with the mark of royalty on him. He had to leave without luggage or food and water. He was heartbroken that he couldn't say goodbye to his parents and explain matters to his benefactor and friend Nkosi, but there was no time. Pharaoh would send chariots after him, arrest him, bring him back, and have him publicly hanged.

Moses was tall and his legs were extremely muscular. He was able to take long strides through the desert. He was young, well-toned, robust, and agile. He made good time and before long he arrived at three Bedouin tents. The leader, a glassy-eyed, underfed man looked at the Egyptian with astonishment. Moses greeted him with a smile. "My good man, I'm willing to trade my gold necklace for food and water." The leader ran into his tent and came out with a bundle of food and a jug of water. "Thank you," Moses said. "I'll be on my way. Please don't tell anyone you met me."

Moses kept pressing on with the goal of reaching the land of Midian. He feared that Pharaoh's chariots might be in close pursuit. When he ran out of food and water, he prayed to God. Suddenly a caravan appeared in front of him.

Moses held up his hand and stopped the first camel. The leader touched the camel's side with a stick and the camel lowered itself to the sand. "I'm Yousef, the chief of this tribe. Why did you stop us?"

"My name is 'Mo,'" Moses said. He didn't want to reveal that he was a prince of Egypt in deep trouble. "I need food and water for I'm on my way to Midian."

"We don't give supplies for nothing," the chief said.

Moses remembered that his mother had taught him not to buy retail and other sensible business practices. "I have two gold bracelets that I'll trade."

The chief said, "Two bracelets will get you one-half pound of dates."

Moses had hidden his heavy gold neck collar. He took it out and displayed it.

"For that useless piece of jewelry that causes neck pain, I will trade you a pint of goat milk, no water."

Moses sighed. "Here are two gold pendants carved with the pictures of an ibis and a camel."

"That's more like it," the leader said. "I will give you a liter of water for them."

"I need food," Moses said. "Here are my gold earrings."

"They are small," the chief said. "They are worth only two loaves of bread."

"I need four loaves of bread," Moses said as he dug into the pocket of his robe and brought out two platinum rings with diamonds.

"Wow," the chief said. "Those rings are real nice. For them I'll give you five loaves of bread and another pound of dates."

When Moses had consumed all the food he had traded for his jewelry, he walked many more land cubits without reaching Midian, which was 2,885 land cubits from the palace. Then when he had run out of water, he prayed to the Lord God and sure enough he spied a tent in the desert. He was able to trade his gold buttons for water and more food. The buttons had held his robe together and it blew apart in the desert wind. Moses had to use his hand to keep his robe closed. By this time he had lost twenty pounds, but he was safe. It was too far for the chariots to find him, but he had another problem. It began with a dance of the wind playing with the sand. The sand in the air became oppressive. Moses looked up at the sky and saw that the brilliant blue sky was taking on a threatening dullness. Sheets of sand began to hurl across the surface of the desert. *Oh boy, I'm in for it now.*

Suddenly Moses spied a lone camel driver. He rushed to his side. "I'm Ahmed," the camel driver said. "We can take shelter lying on my camel's side."

"I'm Moses, and I thank you." *This is a good man. I'm very lucky to have come across him.*

The camel lay down, as the assailing sand whirled around. Ahmed gave Moses a fabric to wind around his head and face. He took another piece of cloth, and he did the same thing for himself. The sun was now completely dimmed and Moses became frightened. His heart beat fast and perspiration ran down his body inside his robe.

Ahmed and Moses and the camel closed their eyes. Even so, the full fury of the sandstorm threatened them. The sand penetrated the men's eyes. Their faces, knees, thighs, and whole bodies were overwhelmed. The hurling blasts of sand searched out every weak spot of their skin. Moses breathed the sand in, ate it, drank it, and hated it. The finest particles penetrated the pores of his skin that had been treated with the most expensive creams when he had been in the palace. The creams had softened his skin until it was satiny smooth like a baby's. They had strengthened it as well, but it was now completely vulnerable.

The storm increased in intensity. Moses heard the hissing sound of the grains increasing in volume. He choked at a lump in his throat. The sand spattered around like pebbles lashing at him. A brief lull in the onslaught helped him take a breath. He huddled next to the shelter of the hairy camel.

Piles of sand kept building up. He coughed from the dust that irritated his lungs and agitated his frayed nerves. This was a stark and terrifying desert filled with sandstorms, vultures, and giant lizards.

Two days later when the sandstorm abated, Moses took off his sandals and said a prayer. "Thank you, Lord God, for my survival through a cataclysmic event. Blessed be your name, King of the Universe, for saving your servant Moses. And blessed be Abraham and Sarah, Isaac and Rebecca, Jacob and Rachel and Leah. The sandstorm could have killed me if I hadn't met Ahmed and his camel. Please bless both of them."

Ahmed heard what Moses had said. "What God do you pray to?"

"I'm a Hebrew and I pray to my God who created all of us, even your camel, may he be healthy."

"Thank you for your prayer and Yloo thanks you too. He's a wonderful animal, my ship in the desert. He's better than any horse, dog, or cat. Where are you headed?"

"I'm going to Midian," Moses said as he flicked off more sand from his arms.

"You travel with nothing. Why?" Ahmed asked with a puzzled expression.

What should I reveal? I'll lie. My mother taught me if you have to lie make sure that some of the lie is the truth. "I come from Egypt where the Hebrews are slaves to Pharaoh. I have escaped and wish to live a life of freedom."

"That is admirable. I cherish my freedom. Yloo and I are going to Midian too. I paint pictures on rocks and I sell my rocks there. When I have enough money for food, I return to the desert. Moses, would you do me the honor of accompanying us?"

Surely the Lord God has sent me a benevolent angel. "Thank you for your generosity. I am in your debt. I accept your offer. I hope that in time I can pay you back."

"That's unnecessary. You see, I talk to Yloo but he doesn't answer. You're human, of course, and I'm grateful for your company."

During the rest of the journey Ahmed kept praising his camel. "Yloo's lips are so thick that sand can't get through. He's able to survive situations that other animals can't."

Moses answered, "The Lord God created such a strong animal and I praise Him for it."

Ahmed said, "Yloo has such solid legs that he can kick a predator and hurt it. It happened one day that a lion came close. Yloo kicked him and the lion ran away. He's most amazing. My father gave him to me when both he and I were six years old. Do you have any animals?"

"I was too busy even to take care of a dog or cat. But I do know how to care for a horse."

"We'll stop here for the night," Ahmed said. "I have dried fruit in a bag that I'll share with you, my newfound friend."

That's how the prince of Egypt and his Bedouin companion spent the next few nights under the starry magnificence of the dry and arid Sinai Desert.

CHAPTER 11

THE CLOSER TO Midian the two new friends came the more excited they felt. Suddenly Moses' face lit up when he spotted a sign that read **ONE THOUSAND LAND CUBITS TO MIDIAN**. He said to Ahmed, "I'm getting camel-sick from the bumping. Please let me down and I'll walk the rest of the way." In biblical times people didn't get car-sick, but they still were susceptible to motion sickness.

Moses walked on the sand until he saw another sign that read **500 LAND CUBITS TO MIDIAN, A FRIENDLY CITY.** He kept going until the next sign that read **250 LAND CUBITS TO MIDIAN, SHOREFRONT PROPERTY AVAILABLE.** Moses trudged on with a song in his heart. The next sign read **YOU HAVE ARRIVED – WE WELCOME YOU TO MIDIAN**.

Ahmed stopped his camel at the main well on the outskirts of the city. He waited fifteen minutes until Moses arrived. Ahmed and Moses were both young bachelors who were interested in young women. They fastened their eyes on seven sister shepherdesses at the well. The tallest of the girls was just an inch shorter than Moses. She was nineteen and dark from the desert sun. The next three girls looked alike and were eighteen. Moses concluded that they were triplets. Two shorter girls also resembled each other. They had to be twins about seventeen. The last girl was as short as Ahmed and looked about sixteen. Moses was attracted to the eldest of the sisters, and Ahmed was entranced by the youngest.

When the girls started to draw water from the well to fill their troughs and water their father's flock, shepherds who were women-haters showed up. The male chauvinist pigs teased the girls. "You silly sisters look like your sheep. Leave this well before we drive you from the face of the earth." The shepherds were so mean that they started to push each girl and knock them down.

When Moses saw this injustice, he became angry. *I had to flee Egypt because of my temper. I better not punch them.* Moses did shove them away, and when Ahmed saw what his friend was doing he joined in the fray.

When the shepherds ran away, both Moses and Ahmed watered the flock. The oldest girl, who was modest, cast her eyes down and thanked them. When she came to her beach home, which was on the east shore of the Gulf of Aqaba northeast of the Red Sea, she told her father how these men had been so kind as to water their flocks after chasing the shepherds away. Her father asked, "What did they look like?"

The eldest daughter said, "One was a tall handsome Egyptian about my age and the other one was a short Bedouin about Seven's age."

The father's name was Jethro and he had been kicked in the head by a cow when he had been a boy. His memory was poor for some things, especially for names though he was a very intelligent man. Therefore, he gave his daughters numbers. The oldest one was One, named Zipporah by her mother after her deceased grandmother, and the others had numbers according to the order of their birth. The triplets were called numbers Two, Three, and Four. Endearingly, the father called them in turn, Tiny Two, Thrilling Three, and Frolicking Four. The twins he called numbers Five and Six—Fancy Five and Saucy Six. The youngest one, Seven, he called Sweet Seven. But the sisters called her Seven for short.

Jethro was a hospitable man. He said to Zipporah, "Where are these men?"

She answered, "I guess they're still at the well. They looked very dirty from the rigors of their journey and they needed to wash themselves."

"Why did you leave them? Didn't I teach you that one kindness deserves another in return?"

"I'm sorry, Father."

"Go back and get them. Bring them to our home and we'll feed them. We'll serve herring and potatoes, gefilte fish with horseradish, bagels and lox, and some kasha knishes. They can feast on the food and drink our wine."

"Yes, Father. I'll do as you say."

"Also, Sweet Seven, make sure you dust all the furniture. There shouldn't be a speck of dust when the men show up." Jethro had been hoping that he could marry off all his daughters because their upkeep was very expensive. He thought there was a possibility that these two men might be interested in marriage, so he might then have only five more marriages to worry about.

"All right, Father. I'll dust thoroughly."

"I want all of you from Number One through Number Seven to put on your best robes, comb your hair, and wash your faces."

"Yes, Father, we will do as you say."

Moses and Ahmed were first shown to the bath where they scrubbed themselves until they glowed with cleanliness. Jethro gave them clean clothes and then introduced them to his wife, a woman who looked worn out from giving birth to the seven daughters. She was depressed that she had not had any sons. Jethro looked at things differently. He was proud of his seven jewels.

After the hearty meal the sisters put on a performance. They danced individually and then together in a circle. Moses kept his eyes on Zipporah and Ahmed couldn't take his eyes off of Sweet Seven. Jethro questioned Moses. "Do you have an occupation?"

"No," Moses said. "I'm not a carpenter, a plumber, or an architect. I would like to stay in Midian, but I need a job; and I may not have skills needed locally."

Jethro clapped his hands. "Since you have chased the shepherds away, I would like you to care for my numerous flocks. I mean flocks of sheep, not of camels. My girls take care of the camels."

"Thank you for offering me employment. I accept. I'll take care of every sheep in your flocks."

Then Jethro turned to Ahmed. "Do you need work, too?"

"No, sir, I'm a painter. I paint rocks and sell them in the market. I'll do this until I have enough to buy supplies, then my camel and I will go back to the desert where my family lives."

Ahmed did as he had said he would, with the exception that he waited until Sweet Seven was eighteen. He asked for her hand, and Jethro was so happy to marry off his daughter that he gladly gave his permission. He gained a son-in-law who was talented as a painter and had a wonderful camel. Sweet Seven, who loved Ahmed, was happy to go with him and live in the desert. The rule was to marry off daughters according to their birth order, but Jethro made an exception in Seven's case, because she and Ahmed were so well suited for each other owing to the shortness of height they had in common.

Moses was full to overflowing with love in his heart for the eldest daughter. Two-and-a-half years later he went to Jethro to ask him for Zipporah's hand in marriage.

"I've been happy to take care of your flocks," Moses said.

"You've been a wonderful shepherd. You never even lost one sheep."

Moses bit down on his lips. He sat down opposite Jethro at the kitchen table. "Does that mean you trust me?"

"Why would you ask such a question? Of course I trust you."

"A shepherd isn't a rich man. Are you looking forward to marrying your daughters to men with money?"

Jethro shook his head. "I consider character more important than money. I would like to see my daughters settled with men who are honest, kind, and have a sense of humor."

Moses looked puzzled. "I don't think I have a sense of humor, but I'm honest and I'm kind. My mother always told me I was a good person."

"Where is your mother? Is she dead?"

"No. My mother lives in Egypt. But I come to you now to ask permission to marry."

Jethro hesitated. "Do you have a particular daughter in mind? You need to choose the oldest one."

Moses nodded, "As a matter of fact, I do love Zipporah the best."

"You may marry her with my blessings," Jethro said smiling as he was ecstatic to give her away. Zipporah liked jewels and clothes and she was "high-maintenance," as they say. Now he could concentrate on marrying off his five other daughters. Soon after that he took a trip to Canaan and brought back five brothers who had been looking for brides, and lo and behold, all his daughters became other men's responsibility. Jethro went around Midian singing and humming. He was a happy man indeed.

CHAPTER 12

ZIPPORAH WAS NOT only a devoted wife to Moses, but she was an outstanding cook and housekeeper. Everything in their house had a place and everything was dusted daily.

One night when Zipporah and Moses were sitting outside their house, Zipporah asked a question. "Which is closer, Egypt or the moon?"

Moses answered, "What do you think?"

"The moon is closer," Zipporah said.

"Why do you say that?"

"I can see the moon, but I can't see Egypt."

Moses smiled and kissed his wife.

"I have good news," Zipporah said. "I'm expecting."

"Expecting guests?" Moses knew what Zipporah meant but he teased her a little.

"No, not guests. I'm expecting a baby. I may have triplets or twins, as they run in my family."

Moses wasn't comfortable with the idea of having multiple births because he wasn't earning too many shekels as a shepherd for his father-in-law, but Moses believed that the Lord God would provide so he didn't worry that much. After nine months Zipporah gave birth to a son.

"What should I name him?" Moses said. "Well, I'm a stranger in a strange land. I shall name our son Gershom which means 'a stranger there.'"

Zipporah said, "That's a strange name. Why don't you name him after your friend Ahmed?"

"Ahmed is a nice name, but I like 'Gershom' better."

"All right," Zipporah said. "Gershom is rhythmical. I'll call him 'Gershom' and I'll teach him to call me 'Mom' since Gershom rhymes with 'Mom'."

"It may take him a year to learn that," Moses pointed out.

"I have patience."

Back in Egypt an angry Pharaoh called for Nkosi. He bellowed, "I want three strong men to search for Moses."

"Yes, My Lord Goodness Gracious. Moses may have taken refuge in the Sinai desert, or he may have even fled to another country."

"I know that," Pharaoh said. "Therefore each man is to learn a different language since Moses could've taken refuge in a county where Egyptian isn't spoken."

"What languages should they learn, My Lord Goodness Gracious?"

"Stop calling me that."

"What should I call you?"

"Call me, Your Majesty."

"Yes, Your Majesty."

"I want one to learn Hebrew, a vile but necessary language. The second will learn Arabic, and the third will learn to speak and understand Midianese."

"What is 'Midianese'?"

"It's the language that is spoken in Midian."

Nkosi thought of something else to delay the spies. "Should they learn to read the language as well, Your Majesty?"

"Not necessary, but when you select the men pick those who are not only strong but smart and quick in learning a new language."

"Do we have teachers who are familiar with these languages, Your Majesty?"

"Egypt is the most advanced country in the world. We have teachers of astronomy, mathematics, architecture, geography, religion, medicine, magic, literature, and languages."

Nkosi selected Femi, Omar, and Lateef. Femi learned Hebrew, Omar studied Arabic, and Lateef put his mind to Midianese.

#

One day when Moses was tending the flock one Egyptian security guard pounded on Jethro's front door. Lateef yelled, "Midianite, open up." Jethro shook with fright. He jerked the door open and with anguish looked at the uniformed, tall, muscular man who pushed his way into his home.

"May I help you, sir?" Jethro asked as his hands shook.

"Give me food and drink," the guard said who spoke a dialect of the Hebrew language called Midianese. He sat down at the table.

Jethro's wife brought bread and water. "You, woman, stay here," Lateef ordered.

When he finished eating, Lateef said, "For years we've been looking for a murderer. He's a Prince of Egypt who fled our country. I'm here under Pharaoh's command to bring him back to Egypt to be hanged."

Jethro trembled. "I know of no Prince of Egypt. My eldest son-in-law is a lowly shepherd. The other five are merchants and the youngest son-in-law is in the Sinai desert with my daughter Seven."

"I'll search your home and if I find Moses I'll kill you."

"You won't find him here," Jethro said. "A Prince wouldn't stay in my humble dwelling."

Lateef, accompanied by other Egyptian guards, searched the house and then the fields. After they left, Jethro put a cold cloth to his forehead. He waited impatiently until Moses came home. "Something terrible has happened when you were out," he said as he wrung his hands.

"What has occurred?"

"A uniformed Egyptian came looking for a man named Moses who he said was a prince of Egypt who is a murderer and who he will bring back to Egypt to be hanged. It can't be you, can it?"

"Yes, it's me. I'm a Hebrew but I was raised by the Princess mother as an Egyptian in the palace. I accidentally killed a taskmaster. Please forgive me for not telling you the truth."

"I'd never betray you," Jethro said. "The man left and I pray he won't come back. Come, let's go for a walk and try to calm down."

They ambled down a path and gravitated to the sea where they sat down on a bench. The salty sea air penetrated Moses' nose. As he breathed in the tangy scent he began to relax. "I know I can trust you. Sometimes I have a nasty temper. In fact, when I was in the palace I was placed in an Anger Management Class."

"Really? I never seen you get angry."

"Most of the time I keep my anger inside."

Jethro shook his head back and forth. "That's not healthy."

"I know but I can't help myself."

"You have to express yourself or you'll wind up with all kinds of physical ailments. Did you learn anything in the Anger Management class?"

"Not really. I hated the class so much that I had to repeat it."

"Why do you think you get so angry?" Jethro asked in a kind voice.

"There are many reasons for my anger. I resented being brought up as an Egyptian when I knew I was a Hebrew. I had to live a lie, and suppress my true feelings. I believe in one God, but I was taught to pray to many gods. As a child I went to bed crying myself to sleep. My adoptive mother, the Princess, allowed me to visit my Hebrew family who showed me love and taught me to believe in one God. I wanted to visit my biological family even more than I had been permitted to do. I was constantly kept busy with all kinds of subjects that I had to learn."

"What are the other reasons you're angry?"

"I saw my people forced into slavery, whipped and tortured, starved until you could see their bones protruding from their emaciated bodies. Who do you think is building the pyramids for Pharaoh?"

"I thought the Egyptians build their own pyramids."

"Sure, years ago, but not now. When I was a baby Pharaoh decreed that all Hebrew male babies were to be killed. I was spared but very many other boy babies were put to death. I have survivor's guilt."

"What's 'survivor's guilt'?"

"It's when a person feels guilty about surviving when others didn't. Not only wasn't I killed, but when the other babies were, I was adopted by the Princess, raised in a palace, and given all the advantages of a royal. I still have nightmares about lying in my basket while boy babies all over Egypt were being killed."

"I'm so sorry," Jethro said as his eyes began to tear. "Moses, it's not your fault that you were a male baby who lived. You have to get over your guilt."

"I can't. It haunts me day and night. When I'm caring for the flock it's in my mind. I know I'm not responsible, but my emotions tell me I am."

"I feel your pain," Jethro said as he placed his hand on Moses' shoulder.

"Something else stirs my anger. It's my hesitant speech. Even though I was given speech lessons, my tongue still doesn't behave. It's like a rock in my mouth. It pains me to remember my childhood. I don't want to talk about it. Instead, let's look up at the starry sky."

"Aha," Jethro said. "Nothing brings out the spiritual side of people than contemplating the stars. They are so lovely. A higher power must've made them for us to admire."

"I think the heavenly bodies have their purpose, but I don't know what it is. Someday after I die I think I'll learn all about them," Moses mused. "When I was a student I had to study astronomy which Egyptians consider sacred. Certain stars are seen in the constellations. For instance, Orion represents Osiris, who was the god of death, rebirth, and the afterlife. Look up at that cluster of stars that resemble milk. The Egyptians say that is the sky goddess Nut who is giving birth to the sun god Ra. I think that strip of milk is stars clustered together."

"You know a lot," Jethro remarked.

"I had to memorize everything about astronomy. See the full moon up there? When something is beautiful, like my wife and your daughter Zipporah, the Egyptians liken the beauty of a woman to the moon. In Egyptian it is said, *"Helwa zay el ammar,"* which means 'beautiful like the moon.'"

"Very poetic," Jethro said. "Tell me more."

"The dog-star *Sopdet* in Egyptian is associated with the goddess Isis. When it rises, it signals the coming of the Nile's inundation."

"Is that important?"

"You better believe it. Without the flooding of the river there wouldn't be farming in Egypt. In fact, Egypt wouldn't even be a country. The Egyptian astronomers are actually priests. They were the ones who recognized that the flooding occurred at the summer solstice. Since the priests were able to predict the annual flooding they became quite powerful."

"You said summer solstice. What does 'solstice' mean?"

"Solstice is the longest day of the year. It's a festival in Egypt. Sopdet is the brightest star in the sky, and the birthplace of Isis. New Year's Day begins at dawn when Sopdet appears on the horizon. It's the shining morning star that emerges from the darkness of the underworld. When Sopdet appears, the Nile floods."

Moses had a dreamy expression. "I remember how the temples were filled with the sounds of the priestesses chanting and playing drums. Waves of joy permeated all over Egypt. The celebration lasted for fourteen days. Even I was caught up in the excitement of New Year's Day. People danced wildly in the streets. They decorated their homes and had feasts of meat and drink. Many people got drunk."

"It sounds like they lost all inhibitions."

"You could say that. Some men drank so much they became drunkards. Even Pharaoh stumbled around."

"What about his wife?"

"Oh, you mean the chief wife? She got drunk too. Pharaoh had a harem but I wasn't allowed in, so I don't know what it looked like or what happened in it."

"Tell me about the pyramids I've heard so much about. Do they have anything to do with the stars?"

"Good question! All of them have astronomical orientations. The horizon is also extremely important since it's there that the sun appears and disappears. I had to memorize a hymn to the sun god. 'Oh Ra! In thine egg, radiant in thy disk, shining forth from the horizon, swimming over the steel firmament.' The hymn goes on and on. I can't remember the rest of the hymn."

"Is the sun always called Ra?"

"No, the morning sun is Horus, the child of Osiris and Isis. The noon sun is Ra because of its great strength. The evening sun is Atum, the creator god who lifts pharaohs from their tombs and brings them to the stars. Have you noticed how red the sun is at sunset?"

"Yes."

"According to the Egyptians the color is considered to be the blood from the sun god as he died. I like the stars but I can't believe in them as gods."

"Ooh, my back hurts," Jethro said as he twisted his face in pain.

"I can help you. You know, when I was learning how to box, after each lesson a male servant would massage my body. I learned how to do this. Why don't we go back to the house and I'll give you a massage?"

"That would be great." Jethro stood back and as he turned around he spotted the Egyptian security guards. In an agitated state he whispered "The Egyptian men are coming after you. Run! Hide!"

Moses wasted no time. He jumped into the sea and started swimming away. It was summer and the water was warm. Moses was a strong swimmer but all he knew was the dog paddle which he learned as a child. This didn't get him very far. Now that he was an adult his muscles were well developed and his legs strong from running after the sheep. He began to keep his spine and head in a straight line. He relaxed his shoulders for optimal reach and moved his arms alternately overhead, keeping his face submerged and coming up for air when it was necessary.

He began to move his arms like a baby crawls. We have to give Moses credit for inventing the swimming crawl position. After he had swum a while he looked behind, and saw that the men were not chasing him. He came ashore breathing a sigh of relief, rested until he felt stronger, and then he started walking to the next town.

He knocked at a door and a wrinkled old woman opened it. "What do you want?" she asked in a whiny voice.

"I'm sorry to bother you," Moses said haltingly and awkwardly. "My horse kicked me and ran away with all my food and my clothing. "I need a place to rest."

"Come in," the gaped-tooth woman said as she held the door open. "I can tell you've been hurt. I have lived alone ever since my husband died twenty years ago."

Moses walked with a limp as he entered a tiny house. The dark sitting room was furnished with two wobbly chairs and a bent table. The hearth was unlit. "Let me get you some nourishment. My name is Mina. What's your name, young man?"

"They call me Mo. Thank you for your gracious hospitality."

"Take a seat at the table, Mo," Mina croaked.

Moses' foot got caught on a torn mat on the earthen floor. As he sat down he cast the mat aside. *I feel sorry for this woman. I never realized that people could be so poor.*

By the time Mina brought in the food Moses was fast asleep with his head on his arm on the table. Mina put the wooden dish and the water jug on the table and left him alone. She checked once more. The food had been eaten and the jug was empty. Moses had woken up and eaten the food, but had fallen asleep again. Mina tiptoed into her bedroom with a smile on her face.

The next morning Moses asked Mina for an axe. He cut away the dead wood and straightened the legs of the table and the chairs. Mina was delighted. "The legs of my bed are also bent," she said.

"I'll take care of them," Moses said. "Do you have any other chores for me? I'd like to stay here as long as I can and I'll help you do things."

Mina smiled. "Thank you. I guess you don't know how to sew, do you?"

"My mother taught me to sew. I've made pillows. What do you want sewn?"

Mina left the room and brought back two robes with rips. "My eyes aren't strong anymore. Could you possibly mend my robes?"

"Just give me your needle and thread and I'll get to work. I love to sew. When I was younger, I wanted to be a tailor, but I later changed my mind."

When Moses was using the backstitch on Mina's robe she asked, "It's not my business, but what's your occupation now?"

"I'm a shepherd. I like to be outdoors and I like sheep. The Lord God made those gentle creatures."

"Who are the gods that you believe in?"

"I believe in just one—the one who made this world and everything and everyone in it. How many gods do you believe in, Mina?"

"I believe in four gods, the god of the sky, the god of the earth, the god of the water, and the god of people. I don't think there is one god because there is too much work for just one to take care of."

"I understand," Moses said. "You're a religious woman and a kind one."

Moses remained in Mina's house for six days before he returned to Midian. Zipporah and Jethro were both overjoyed to see him. "The men who were after you haven't returned to Egypt. They're still searching for you," Jethro said. "They've searched every house and even scoured the fields. You need to leave here immediately. Drive the flock to the mountain where there is more grass and let them feed."

"Don't go yet," Zipporah said. "Wait until I prepare food and drink for you. Your sheep may be hungry, but how about you? Don't you want to keep your stomach full?"

"I will wait, Zipporah, but make it snappy."

I, Methuselah, told you that in biblical times they had no radio, television, or automobiles, but they did use carrier pigeons to get news. While Moses was waiting impatiently for his food Jethro said, "I sent my carrier pigeon to Egypt and it returned with a disturbing message."

"Is Pharaoh killing more Hebrews?" Moses asked.

"The Pharaoh is oppressing the Hebrews even more. They are building a temple to honor the last Pharaoh. The work is backbreaking and your people are suffering."

"I wish I could do something to help them," Moses said. He left with a huge bag of food and drink. It was so heavy he had a hard time carrying it. As he led the sheep to Horeb, the mountain of God, later to be known as Mount Sinai, he worried about the fate of the Hebrews in Egypt. That night he had a nightmare. Pharaoh's Hebrew slaves were dropping dead like flies.

The next morning Moses continued on his journey to Mt. Horeb and when he approached it he noticed a bush that was on fire. *No one has rubbed two sticks together to light a fire. Why is the bush burning?* Moses expected the fire might spread to his sheep, but it didn't. The bush kept burning but it remained a bush. *I can't understand why it doesn't burn up. It's against the law of physics.*

Then suddenly Moses heard a voice. The Lord God said, "Moses, Moses," like He wanted Moses to pay close attention.

I better answer Him.

In biblical times they didn't have GPS and Moses wasn't sure if God knew exactly where he was. He didn't quite say, 'Here am I' like it says in the Bible but with a loud voice he said, "I'm right here."

Then God said, "Don't come any closer. You are standing on holy ground. Take off your shoes."

Immediately Moses removed his sandals with his clammy hands. He was glad that that morning he had taken a bath.

The Lord God saw Moses' bare feet so He continued identifying himself. "I'm the God of thy fathers, the God of Abraham, the God of Isaac, and the God of Jacob."

Moses trembled with fear. He covered his face with both hands for he was afraid to look upon God.

The Lord God spoke again. "I have seen the affliction of my people in Egypt. I have heard their cries and their sorrows that are caused by the taskmasters. I want to bring them out of Egypt to a good and large land that is flowing with milk and honey." God was referring to the milk from goats and honey from dates.

Moses took a deep breath. He had a hunger for justice, for righteousness, and for truthfulness.

The Lord God continued talking. "The place I mean is the land of the Canaanite, the Hittite, the Amorite, the Perizzite, the Hivite, and the Jebusite."

It's amazing that the Lord God knows about all these peoples.

Then God said something that caused Moses to get dizzy and almost faint. He said, "I will send thee unto Pharaoh, that thou mayest bring forth my people, the children of Israel out of Egypt."

Moses was speechless. *Me? He wants **me** to go to Pharaoh and bring out my brethren? Impossible. I'm just a shepherd, a nobody, a nothing, a shlemiel. I can't even talk properly. But I have to answer.* "Who am I that I should go to Pharaoh to bring forth the children of Israel from Egypt?" *I sure hope the Lord God listens to what I'm saying. I think He's about to make a big mistake.*

God said, "For sure I will be with you. When you have brought my people out of Egypt, you shall serve Me on this mountain."

And Moses thought he was having a hallucination from the hot sun beating down on his head. *I should not have forgotten to take my sun hat. I'm losing my sanity for certain. God would never send me to Pharaoh. I better play along with this megalomania and play it out to the end.* "When I come to the children of Israel, who should I say sent me? They're sure to ask for Your name."

God's booming voice cried out, "Just say **I AM THAT I AM.** Say **I AM** sent me to you. The Lord God of your fathers, the God of Abraham, the God of Isaac, and the God of Jacob has sent me to you. Go now and gather the elders of Israel and tell them that God has appeared to you and has seen the affliction you are suffering in Egypt." God repeated again what He had said before because He wanted to make His point clearly.

Oh boy! Maybe I'm not delusional. Could it be the bush isn't a visual hallucination? Could it be that God's voice isn't an auditory hallucination?

The Lord God continued talking, "You shall go to the king of Egypt and ask him to let my people go to the wilderness after a three day's journey so that they may sacrifice to Me."

This won't work! Pharaoh will never listen to me.

"Furthermore," God said, "I am certain Pharaoh will not let you go, but I will work wonders and it will come to pass that the king will let you go. From Egypt you shall take jewels of silver and gold, and raiment, and you shall despoil Egypt."

That's a lot to take in. The Lord God wants me to steal. I'm not a crook. I wonder if it'll come to pass. "They won't believe me or listen to me. They'll say that the Lord hasn't appeared before you."

The Lord then asked as if He didn't know, "What's in your hand?" He had the habit of asking questions that He knew the answer to, like when He had asked Cain where his brother was.

Moses answered, "It's a staff I use for my sheep."

"Cast the staff on the ground," God said.

Moses did as he was ordered and the staff turned into a serpent. Moses recognized the serpent as a rattlesnake. He became very frightened and backed away ten cubits from the serpent.

"Come back," God said. "Grab the serpent by the tail."

Moses' knees shook as he managed to keep away from the serpent's mouth and snatched it by the tail even as the serpent spun around to strike him.

God said, "Now shake the serpent."

Moses arms trembled as he shook the reptile with all his strength and once again it became a staff. *Whew, I hope the Lord God doesn't give me any more tricks like this to perform.*

"Now put your hand in your bosom." He said "bosom," but He meant "chest."

Moses slid his hand under his robe and placed it on the skin of his chest. When he took it out, it was leprous, as white as an egg. Moses gritted his teeth and held his hand away from his body.

God said, "Now put your hand back into your bosom." *Does God really mean this? If I do this, surely the leprosy will spread all over my body.*

Moses hesitated.

God said, "Go ahead, and do not be afraid. Put your hand back in."

Moses shivered. He put his hand on the skin of his chest and it became as smooth as before without any sign of leprosy.

Then God said, "If Pharaoh does not take these two signs seriously, nor listen to what you say, then you shall take water from the river and pour it on the land and the river shall turn to blood."

"Ooh!" Moses said. "I have an-another ob-objection. I'm a slow talker with a speech de-defect that I haven't overcome. My Lord God, can't you pick someone else?"

"No, I select who I choose. I will teach you what to say."

"I'm not sure I can do it," Moses said shaking his head.

By this time God got angry at Moses for his stalling. He said, "Is not Aaron the Levite your brother? I know he speaks well. You will tell him what to say and he will be your spokesman. Now take your staff in your hand, for you shall do the signs that I showed you. Do you remember the signs?"

"Yes, I do. The first one is the staff turning into the reptile and back again. The second one is my hand becoming leprous after I put it under my robe on my chest. Then I put it back and I'm healthy again. The third one is water from the river in Egypt that turns to blood on the land."

"Good. I did give you a remarkable memory," God said proudly.

CHAPTER 13

MOSES THOUGHT ABOUT the miraculous happenings and became convinced he wasn't having hallucinations. He returned home with his flock.

Jethro was smiling when he saw his son-in-law. "The Egyptian men left last week. You're safe now."

"I don't know about that," Moses said. "I have to go to Egypt."

"I don't understand."

"God spoke to me and told me to return there."

"You'll be killed as soon as you set foot in Egypt."

"No I won't. God will take care of me. He has a job for me."

Jethro was a wise understanding man. "Then, Moses, go back to Egypt in peace. Good luck and God bless."

Then the Lord God spoke again, reminding Moses to go to Egypt. He reassured Moses that the men who wanted to kill him were dead.

Moses didn't want to be alone. By now he had another son. He put his wife and sons on a donkey and they traveled through the desert for many days. Moses dreaded a sandstorm, but the weather was clear and he didn't feel so nervous this time. He was anxious to get this part of his life over with. He had really liked being a shepherd in Midian because there hadn't been stress on him there. He had been leading a life without pressure.

The Lord God warned Moses that when he comes to Pharaoh and does the wonders that he was told to do, Pharaoh's heart would get hardened and he wouldn't let the people go. He told Moses to warn the king of Egypt that if he wouldn't free the people Pharaoh would lose his first born. It was a dire warning. Centuries later people sang the song, "Go down, Moses. Way down in Egypt land. Tell old Pharaoh to let my people go. Da, da, da, da."

After Ahmed married Sweet Seven they journeyed to the desert. Seven had the soul of a business woman ever though she was young. She said to Ahmed, "I think we should open an inn and call it Ahmed's Inn."

"I don't know anything about running an inn."

"You'll learn. I'm sure it's not too hard."

"What will I do?"

"Ahmed, you'll decorate it with your art."

"What will you do?"

"I promise I will keep it clean. I'll do all the cooking. I'm really a good cook. I know how to make a positively delicious mushroom and barley soup."

"I'm not sure I can build an inn. I'm just a good camel driver."

"Your family can help you build it. You can paint scenes on all the walls. We can dress Yloo in an outrageous costume and charge people to take camel rides. We'll become prosperous. Please do this for me."

Six months later Ahmed's inn was finished and furnished. He painted beautiful desert landscapes on the walls in the dining room. He painted a starry sky in all the bedrooms. He was such a talented artist that people came from far and wide to see the pictures of the sky and the landscapes of the desert in bloom. The inn became famous—even people from surrounding lands came to see it.

This was the inn that Moses stopped at for a break. Ahmed embraced his long lost friend. He was dressed in exquisite garments. "How are you, my friend?" Ahmed asked with concern in his voice.

"I'm all right—so is Zipporah. We have a newborn son and an older son too. Do you and Seven have children?"

"Yes, we have four daughters. Seven is pregnant and I'm hoping for a boy to help me run my inn. I'd like to call it Ahmed & Son Inn. Would you like to see Yloo? I bet he remembers you."

"I'd love to see him. He saved our lives during the sandstorm."

Ahmed led Moses to the back of the inn where Yloo was eating hay. "Yloo, remember me?" Moses said.

Yloo stopped eating and came over to Moses. Tears dropped from Moses's eyes as he petted the camel on his head. Yloo started baying. It sounded like a deep prolonged howl— something like a sick ram's horn. "I love you too," Moses said as he stroked the camel's head.

"Yloo certainly remembers you, Moses. Can you stay with us for a while? Tell me, where are you off to?"

"I can't stay more than a night. The Lord God told me to go to Egypt to help free my people from bondage."

"Egypt? Aren't you afraid they'll kill you there?"

"No. My God will protect me."

"I don't know about that. He didn't protect you that much before. You almost died in the desert."

"Almost doesn't count. I know you don't believe in my God but He is all powerful and I have faith in Him."

"I wish you could stay longer," Ahmed said sadly. "I'll show you to your room. It's the best in the house."

And this was the inn where Moses and Zipporah had their first disagreement.

When the babies were sleeping, Zipporah said, "I think we should stay here a few days so that you can circumcise our infant and introduce him into being a true Hebrew."

Moses got uptight. He didn't want to cut his infant in his delicate part and cause him pain, but he wasn't forthright with his wife. Moses cried disingenuously, "The Lord God wants us to go to Egypt without delay. There is no time now for a circumcision. It can be done in Egypt when my family is there and we can make a party with wine and halvah."

"What's halvah?" Zipporah asked.

"You never heard of halvah? It's a soft candy made out of sesame paste. You'll love it. Let's forget about the circumcision for now."

Zipporah said, "I think you're making a big mistake."

Moses's face turned red. "I don't make mistakes. I don't like to be criticized. You're being bossy and that makes me mad."

Zipporah looked at her husband with scorn in her dark eyes. "I'm not bossy. I'm telling you the truth. Besides, I thought you learned something from that Anger Management class in Egypt you told me about. You'll be sorry if you won't listen to me."

Zipporah's words did come true. Moses should've listened to his wise wife. The Lord God was so annoyed with him that He would've sent an angel to kill him if Zipporah hadn't taken matters into her own hands. She picked up a stone and sharpened it with another stone. Then she gave her baby a few drops of wine on his tongue. She cut off the foreskin of the infant and threw it at Moses' feet crying, "This is what you should've done, my husband."

Moses was so upset he buried his head in his hands. "I had no idea you were planning to do this."

"It had to be done."

"I guess so, but our poor baby. He's crying so much it hurts my heart."

Zipporah said, "It hurts me more than it hurts you, but the Lord God commanded that it be done. It makes our son an Israelite."

Zipporah touched the foreskin to her husband's feet hoping that the blood would save Moses from the Angel of Death. She said, "You are my bridegroom of blood."

"What do you mean?" Moses asked.

"I mean that the baby's blood could have caused your death, but because I did it and the commandment has been observed, your life is spared."

"I shouldn't have waited. But I had another reason. I thought if I circumcised the infant he would be in danger from traveling within three days after the procedure."

"I didn't want you to die. I love you very much so I hardened myself and performed my duty. Hold our baby now and rock him to sleep."

"I love you, my wife. You have taken the Hebrew commandments to heart and that pleases me. Go to sleep. I'll rock the baby." *I should've performed the circumcision. I'm sorry that Zipporah had to do it. It must be harder for a mother who has carried her baby for nine months to cut him and hear him cry with pain. There is no way for me to thank her. I'm so lucky that she's my wife. I have to admit there are times when wives are wiser than husbands.*

#

The Lord then spoke to Aaron, "Go to the wilderness and meet Moses."

Aaron never considered that he was having an auditory hallucination. He did as the Lord God commanded. He met his brother on Mount Horeb—also known as Mount Sinai—and they kissed, hugged, and cried with joy for two hours. Moses told Aaron what God had said. It took an hour to bring Aaron fully up-to-date on all that had happened.

"Where do we go from here?" Aaron asked.

"We have to get prepared for you to talk to Pharaoh in Egyptian."

"I'll never learn Egyptian," Aaron said, as his face fell.

"I'm going to write a Hebrew-Egyptian dictionary. That will take me a month. Then I'll teach you the language in another month."

"You're the educated one in our family. You speak many languages but I only speak Hebrew," Aaron pointed out.

"You're just as intelligent as me. You haven't been exposed to languages. I'm a good teacher and I guarantee you you'll be speaking Egyptian in a very short time."

Moses took a scroll of papyrus and wrote the first Hebrew-Egyptian syllabary. A syllabary is a dictionary of symbols. The one Moses wrote contained common everyday words like *arm, blind, carry, down, end, finger, great, hear, ibis, justice, king, light, mish-mash, no, oath, pitfall, queen, room, sanctity, thirst, undependable, vex, woe, xenophobia, yes,* and *zodiac*.

After Moses completed his dictionary, he began to speak to Aaron in Egyptian. Aaron kept shaking his head. In Hebrew he said, "I have no idea what you're talking about."

"Okay, I'll teach you from scratch."

"I'm willing to learn but slow down, brother."

"Come here," Moses said in Egyptian. He motioned with his hand for Aaron to come closer.

"What are you doing?" Aaron asked. "Are you chasing a mosquito?"

Finally Moses gave up. When we meet Pharaoh, I will talk first in Hebrew, then I'll translate what I have to say in Egyptian, and you'll repeat it in Egyptian. I think that's the best plan."

"Your speech isn't so terrible," Aaron said. "You can talk directly to Pharaoh and I'll stay home."

"Not a good idea," Moses objected. "God agreed to have you speak for me."

"But my Egyptian sounds like I have rocks in my mouth. I stumble more than you."

"Go home and practice," Moses said.

Aaron loved Moses with all his heart and soul. When he entered his home, his older sons, Nadab and Abihu were quarreling. Aaron was a peacemaker and he settled their differences. "Shake hands, boys," he said. The brothers pouted, but they did shake each other's hand.

Aaron's younger sons, Eleazar and Ithamar, were chasing each other around the kitchen table. Eleazar shouted, "Give me back my favorite rock, you thief."

Ithamar stuck out his tongue. "It's my rock. Come and get it."

Aaron felt a headache coming on. "Boys," he said, "I need peace and quiet because I have to study the Egyptian language."

Eleazar and Ithamar stopped in their tracks. Ithamar said, "Father, are we moving to Egypt proper from Goshen?"

"No, we're not moving."

Ithamar asked, "So why do you have to study Egyptian?"

"It's a long story," Aaron said. "I'll tell it to you another time."

Elisheba, Aaron's wife entered the house carrying a jug of water. "What's doing, dear?" she asked.

"Moses asked me to learn Egyptian because the Lord God told him to go to Egypt to ask Pharaoh to free our people."

"Then why do *you* have to learn Egyptian?"

"You know that Moses is slow of speech. He asked me to be his mouthpiece and I agreed."

"Would you like me to help you?"

"That's okay by me. I need as much help as I can. The word for 'person' in Egyptian is *'skhks,'* and that's hard to pronounce."

Elisheba nodded in agreement. Keep saying it over and over. What's the next word?"

"It's 'house' which is '*mnzl*'."

"That's no better. Is there any word that's easier?"

Aaron looked at Moses' dictionary. "Here's one. It's '*el maa*' for 'water'."

"I'll be back a little later. I have to cook supper. Keep practicing and you'll be the best mouthpiece in all the land."

I, Methuselah, am aware how hard it was for Aaron to speak to Pharaoh. He's not given the credit for what he deserves.

"Let's first go to meet the elders of the children of Israel. You'll tell them," Moses said, "what I told you. When you speak Hebrew you sound better than I do. I ask you to be my official spokesman."

Moses still wasn't sure that the elders would believe that God had spoken to him, but they were impressed when Moses performed the signs with the staff that turned into a snake and the hand that became leprous. Their hearts led them to pray and bow their heads.

Then Moses said to Aaron, "Now that we're back in Egypt we have to take the next step."

"What should we do?" Aaron asked.

"We need to bathe and dress in fashionable clothes. You look like you need pomade on your hair. I should get a haircut. We have to make a good impression on Pharaoh. Don't talk Hebrew to me. I'll speak in Egyptian, and you can follow my lead and do the same."

Nkosi came out to meet Moses and Aaron. Moses watched as Nkosi moved carefully holding onto a staff for support. His hair had turned as pure white as sheep's wool. "I'm so happy to see you again," Nkosi said as he embraced his protégé.

"I'll never forget your kindness to me," Moses answered. "And now I have to ask you to help me because I've come to persuade Pharaoh to let my people go."

"What do you need me to do?" Nkosi asked.

"My brother and I shall go before Pharaoh and we would appreciate a change of clothes, for, as is said, clothes make the man."

"No problem," Nkosi said. "I'm a rich man. Come to my home and select whatever you wish."

In Nkosi's house Moses chose a garment of white linen. He opted for sandals decorated with gold. Around his neck he hung a neckpiece of gold links and bound his dark hair with a thin band of gold. At his waist he placed an ivory dagger in a golden scabbard. Aaron got dressed too, but in a simpler fashion.

After Moses and Aaron were ready to go, Moses said a special prayer asking the Lord God to help him. When they came to the palace gate, the guards stopped them. One guard asked, "What gifts are you bringing to Pharaoh?"

Moses translated what the guard said to his brother. Aaron said in halting Egyptian, "We're bringing the word of God."

"What? Just words? You can't enter."

God saw how they were blocked and He cleared a path for them. They went to the head of the line in the throne room. Moses walked on the balls of his feet as if he was prepared to lunge forward.

Pharaoh looked at them with disdain. "What do you want?" he asked in Egyptian.

Moses translated and told Aaron to say in Egyptian, of course, "My Lord, the God of Israel says to let my people go so that they may have a feast dedicated to our God in the wilderness."

Pharaoh said to Moses, "Aaron speaks Egyptian with a terrible accent. I never heard my language spoken so terribly." He added, "Your people aren't going anywhere, in fact I'll make them work even harder than before. There's a new obelisk that needs to be built."

Haltingly Aaron said, "Our God wants us to go only on a three day's journey to sacrifice to Him." He didn't remember how to say 'three' so he held up three fingers.

Pharaoh pointed at Moses and Aaron. "Not only can't you speak Egyptian well, you don't recognize that I am the chief god, and I won't let you go. In fact, I want your people to gather straw yourselves for your bricks."

"What did he say?" Aaron asked Moses.

"He said he's the main god and we can't go to the wilderness. He ordered that now the Hebrew slaves have to gather straw to make the bricks. The Israelites won't be given straw anymore."

"That's awful," Aaron said in Hebrew.

"Yes, it is."

"I don't know what you're talking about," Pharaoh said. "Translate every word."

Aaron said in Egyptian, "'*Rah meod*', means 'very bad' or 'awful' in Hebrew."

Moses repeated it in Egyptian, "My brother used the word 'awful'."

A man standing in back of Moses nudged him with his staff. "What is it?" Moses asked.

"You're talking too much. You've been here too long. I have a pound of dates to give to Pharaoh," the man spoke with an annoyed expression.

"Listen, Buster, this is important stuff we're discussing. Wait your turn," Moses said shaking his finger at the rude man. "Besides, Pharaoh doesn't need your dates."

"My name ain't 'Buster,' and you and your mouthpiece better leave now. There's a long line in back of me and you better get moving."

"All right," Moses said, "But we're coming back and we won't leave so quickly the next time."

#

Pharaoh was as good as his word because the very next day the taskmasters forced the Hebrews to forage for straw to make the bricks. "Make them work harder than ever," Pharaoh said.

The Children of Israel became very disheartened. They blamed Moses for asking for three days off. Actually they were good workers, but most of what they constructed got torn down, and work without a purpose was quite discouraging. Some Hebrews worked on the pyramid which was to be the intended home for Pharaoh after he would move to the next world. They buried their own dead in the earth and couldn't comprehend why the king of Egypt needed such a large burial chamber.

Moses returned to the Lord God and said, "I have questions. Why are You doing such evil to your people? Why have You sent me to redeem them? When I went to Pharaoh to ask him to let my people go, why did he make it harder for them? Why have You not delivered our people as You said You would?"

God said, "You have asked me four questions and I will take My time in answering. I'm YHWH, God Almighty. I will give the Children of Israel the land of Canaan. I have heard their groaning and seen their suffering. Tell them I will keep my promise, but in My own good time and for My own reasons. I have selected you as my messenger. I ask you to go before Pharaoh again." Then God made sure that Moses knew that He was aware of all the names of the tribes and their descendants. I, Methuselah, don't need to list them at this point. You can find them in the Bible.

When Moses first fled from Egypt, he was twenty years old and his brother Aaron was twenty-three. Six decades had passed since that time. When a man is sixty now, he's almost ready to retire, but Moses still was in his prime. Both brothers were strong from exercising, walking a thousand land cubits every day. They slept eight hours a night, and they ate healthful meals. Both men were faithful to their wives and caring fathers to their children.

God spoke to Moses and Aaron, "Go to Pharaoh once again. This time Aaron shall cast down his staff in front of Pharaoh and his servants and the staff will turn into a serpent."

They went as bidden and the guards at the gate of the palace did not stop them. When they were in the throne room, they saw that no other subjects were around—just Pharaoh, Mrs. Pharaoh, and a dozen servants. Pharaoh was eating an orange. He spat the pits into a decorated bowl that one servant held. The decoration on the bowl was the *ka* or the human spirit represented by two arms reaching upward, although with only two fingers on each hand.

Pharaoh laughed and said, "It's you again. What do you want now?"

Moses and Aaron kept silent. Aaron cast down his staff. Suddenly the staff turned into a writhing rattlesnake that hissed and turned its head hither and fro.

Pharaoh looked at it without fear. "I see you've been practicing magic tricks," he said. He turned to his chief servant. "Send for my wise men and sorcerers and they'll show these brothers a thing or two."

A dozen magicians showed up, each carrying a staff that they cast down. The staffs turned into serpents. Now there were twelve slippery treacherous serpents on the marble floor turning this way and that. Pharaoh left his throne. His servants moved the throne back two cubits to escape the snakes' lethal bites. Mrs. Pharaoh raced out of the throne room screaming, "I hate snakes. Get rid of the beasts." The servants also ran out. Even Moses and Aaron stepped back. A minute passed and nothing happened.

Then Aaron's snake, which was twice the size of the others, swallowed the dozen serpents.

Pharaoh said, "You're trying to frighten me, but it's not working. It's all fake stuff done with mirrors. What are you going to do next? Do you have a card trick? Are you going to make a woman disappear?"

Aaron said in halting Egyptian, "Let my people go."

"Are you crazy?" Pharaoh said. "Just because of one fake trick, you expect me to let my slaves go? I need them to build temples, pyramids, cities, roads, and obelisks. Your people make good slaves. Your people are my servants. You still speak Egyptian with a terrible accent. You're stupid if you think I'll ever change my mind. I'm the main god and what I say goes."

"You'll change your little foolish mind," Moses said in Hebrew.

"What did you say?" Pharaoh demanded to know.

Moses stood tall as he translated the Hebrew into Egyptian. "I said that you'll change your mind."

"No, I won't," Pharaoh said as he picked up a lemon, bit into it, and spit it out.

CHAPTER 14

THE LORD GOD spoke to Moses again. "Tomorrow morning go to the Nile River with Aaron. Pharaoh's heart hardened and Aaron needs to speak to him and ask him to let the children of Israel go."

I'm glad God didn't tell me to go to the palace this time. I like the outdoors, especially the Nile where my adoptive mother found me and I learned to do the dog paddle. I used to see ships sailing upstream from the sea and large rafts with bulrushes drifting down from Upper Egypt.

The next morning Moses and Aaron walked the path to the Nile. Moses pointed, "I see Pharaoh bathing in the river."

"Yes," Aaron said. "But look he's surrounded by his security guards. We won't be able to approach him."

"Yes, we will. God didn't ask us to go here if we wouldn't be able to talk to Pharaoh. You need to have more faith, brother."

When Pharaoh left the river and was drying off, he noticed Moses and Aaron. "You again? I'm tired of seeing your bearded faces. Get going."

Aaron said, "Let my people go." By this time he had memorized it in better-accented Egyptian.

Pharaoh answered, "Never."

Moses said in Hebrew to Aaron, "Repeat after me." Then he spoke in Egyptian, "My Lord God will afflict you now when I put my staff in the water and turn the water to blood."

Aaron said to Moses, "Please repeat what you said. I can't remember all of it."

Moses repeated the sentence. Aaron spoke to Pharaoh and Pharaoh put his hands over his ears and didn't hear a word.

Aaron put his staff in the water and slowly but surely the water turned to blood. Pharaoh stepped away from the river saying, "You think you're a magician, but this isn't blood. You put red dye into the water. My magicians will turn the river back to normal. I'm not letting your people go."

Moses spoke to God and said, "Pharaoh is as stubborn as a donkey."

"I will take care of him," God said. "Tell Aaron to take his staff and stretch it out over the water. Then the streams, the rivers, the ponds, the pools, and the drinking water will all turn to blood."

"Wow," Moses said, after Aaron had accomplished this miracle. The fish died and all the Egyptians were thirsty and had no water to drink. Still and all Pharaoh didn't listen to the word of the Lord God even when the stink of the river spread over the land. For seven days there was no water to be found in all of Egypt.

A newly married Egyptian couple, Siptah and his wife Tausert, had wine and beer left over from their wedding. The water in their jugs had turned to blood so when they were thirsty they drank the alcoholic liquids and got drunk. Siptah, who was a gentle man, turned surly and chased his wife around the kitchen table. She was young and ran like a deer and they both collapsed into a pile on the mud floor with their arms around each other.

"Moses, go back to Pharaoh in his palace," the Lord God said, "And tell him if he does not change his mind, I will send frogs all over the land. They will gather in his bed, in his harem, in his kitchen, and in all his chariots."

Pharaoh didn't listen, and the frogs surely came.

By now Siptah and Tausert had water to drink, but another plague quickly descended upon them. When Tausert went to bed, she cried out in desperation, "There are frogs in my bed. Help me get rid of them."

Siptah rushed in and grabbed the frogs that had landed on Tausert's long black hair. He threw them on the dirt floor and they jumped into the water jug. He ran out of the house and knocked at the neighbor's door. A boy of nine answered screaming, "There are frogs in my cereal."

Siptah went home and held Tausert in his arms while the frogs invaded every corner of the bedroom and the whole house. There were frogs all over Upper and Lower Egypt.

Pharaoh then sent for Moses and Aaron and said in a pleading voice, "Please ask the Lord to remove the frogs and I'll let your people go."

Moses and Aaron stepped over the frogs until they reached the throne where eighty-eight frogs were sitting on the throne croaking. They had to raise their voices so Pharaoh could hear them. "Tomorrow the frogs will be gone." Stepping over the frogs, they then left the palace.

The following day all the frogs died and the people buried them in the sand. When Pharaoh saw that his land was cleared of frogs, he changed his mind and wouldn't let the Hebrews go.

"I knew Pharaoh was stubborn and thick-skinned," Aaron said to Moses. "I don't think he'll ever free our people."

"Have faith," Moses said. "Someday Pharaoh will change his mind, and all the Israelites will leave Egypt."

The next day God said to Moses and Aaron, "This time you do not have to go to the palace. Pharaoh's heart has hardened again. I want Aaron to stretch out his staff. You will see the result."

Moses and Aaron wondered what would happen now. Moses thought God might kill the birds. Aaron thought God might turn the water into wine. But when Aaron stretched out his staff this time, lice invaded the land—except in Goshen where the Hebrews lived. All the dust in the land of Egypt became lice. Lice are wingless insects that love to get onto people's scalps and draw their blood. God had created them to bring trouble to the Egyptians and make them keep scratching their heads and not be able to work. Pharaoh's servants kept plucking lice one by one off of Pharaoh's bald scalp.

"Call my magicians to my side," Pharaoh ordered. When the magicians tried to rid Egypt of the lice, they were unsuccessful. They said, "This is the finger of God who is stronger than you." Pharaoh became so enraged with their heretical assumption he had the chief magician killed and he imprisoned the rest of them.

When the magicians were in prison with their rabbits, the tallest one whose name was Rho said to the others, "Moses has a god who is stronger than Ra. He will prevail. Don't worry. Eventually we'll be released."

"No god is stronger than Ra," the magician named Stu said. "We won't be released until we all pray to Ra. Get down and your knees and start praying."

"I no longer believe in our gods," Rho said.

"Get down on your knees," Stu said.

"I have arthritis in my knees. I can't get down and I won't get down and you can't make me. Besides you were never a good magician. You couldn't make even one rabbit come out of a hat."

"How dare you say that," Stu said as his face reddened like the sun. "I'm a better magician than you ever were. You couldn't do the advanced card tricks."

"I could too."

Stu pushed Rho. Rho pushed him back. It turned into pushing, slapping, pulling, and cursing. The jailer had to separate them and they landed in cells in solitary with no one to talk to. The only company they had were their rabbits.

The next day the Lord God said to Moses, "It is time you went back to Pharaoh since he has not changed his mind. Go in the morning when he will be bathing in the Nile trying to get rid of the lice. Tell him to let My people go to serve Me, or else swarms of flies will be all over Egypt." Flies are germy insects that have wings and settle on food when they need to eat. In biblical times people didn't have insect spray, just numerous fly swatters.

Then Moses and Aaron went back to Pharaoh and told him about the swarms of flies that were on their way. "They'll be all over your house," Aaron said with emphasis, "and your people's houses, but not in Goshen where my people are. Let my people go."

Pharaoh kept waving his hands around his body to stop the flies from landing but there were so many he couldn't chase them away. He couldn't eat and he couldn't sleep. "Are you still up?" Mrs. Pharaoh asked.

"I can't sleep," Pharaoh said, as he slapped his face and his chest.

"Please I beg you to tell Moses to get rid of these pests."

"I won't give in to them because of tiny flies. Flies don't bite like mosquitoes. I have my pride," Pharaoh said.

"Pride goeth before a fall and before swarms of flies," Mrs. Pharaoh said. "Your children are also covered with these buzzing flies. They can't sleep and neither can I. Just send for Moses and speak to him in a nice polite way for a change."

"You're asking me to be polite to my enemy? You have some nerve, woman."

"Don't call me 'woman'. Now you're not even polite to me."

"Sorry! I'm just a nervous wreck."

Pharaoh relented and sent for Moses and Aaron.

"I'll let you go to sacrifice to your God in the wilderness, only don't go too far, and make sure you get rid of these bothersome miserable flies. Tell me, when you're in the wilderness, what will you be doing?"

"We'll pray to our God and offer Him a sacrifice."

"What kind of sacrifice?"

"We use a ram."

Pharaoh's face turned as white as alabaster. "You can't do that," he cried. "The ram is Khnum, the god of the source of the Nile. I will not let you go and desecrate my religion."

Moses and Aaron looked at each other wondering how to proceed when Mrs. Pharaoh said to her husband, "Don't worry so much. Khnum will strike them dead if they use a ram as a sacrifice."

Pharaoh hung his head. "All right go ahead and do your thing, but you'll be sorry."

Moses spoke to God and God removed the flies. Can you guess what happened after that? You better believe it—Pharaoh changed his mind again.

Then God said to Moses, "Go back to the palace and tell Pharaoh to let My people go. If Pharaoh refuses, I have another plague which he has not had before. It's the fifth one and he is going to hate it. It's called 'murrain'."

Moses wrinkled his forehead. "What's 'murrain'?"

"It is an infectious disease that will kill the horses, the donkeys, the camels, the oxen, the cats, and the dogs."

"Pharaoh certainly won't like that."

CHAPTER 15

MOSES LOVED ANIMALS, especially domestic kinds like the gentle sheep he had cared for as a shepherd. He couldn't plead with God to find another way to affect Pharaoh's heart, but he wished he could.

"When will you do that?" Moses asked.

"Tomorrow. The animals that are in Goshen will not be harmed. Only the Egyptian animals will die."

The next morning when Tausert's cat was in bed with her he didn't move. "Sippy," Tausert called. She had stopped calling him 'Siptah', which he didn't like but didn't object to, and shortened his name to 'Sippy'. When he came in, he was carrying his pet dog. "My dog is dead," he cried.

"I think my cat is dead, too," Tausert moaned. "Go next door and see if the neighbors' animals are dead."

Siptah came back with the report that all the sheep and cattle had died. "The Hebrew God has cursed us. I hope Pharaoh will let them leave. We don't need them."

All the Egyptians wept when all their domestic animals died. You would surmise that Pharaoh would then give in to the demands of the Hebrews, but he didn't.

Moses returned to Pharaoh and warned him of the coming sixth plague, but to no avail.

The Lord God had told Moses to sprinkle ashes toward heaven. "You shall do this in front of Pharaoh," He said.

Moses went to the furnace, took some ashes, and put them in an undecorated bowl that his mother had made. He took two handfuls and threw the ashes towards the sky. The ashes, unbelievably, spread to dust all over Egypt. What did the dust do then? It caused boils to sprout on man and whatever beasts happened to have survived. For some reason the crocodiles in the Nile weren't affected.

Pharaoh released his magicians from prison and asked them to remove the painful boils on his body, and when they couldn't and they got the boils themselves, he put them back behind bars.

Siptah looked so ugly with the boils all over his body that Tausert shut herself in the closet and wouldn't come out. "You have boils too," Siptah shouted through the closed door.

"Not as horrible looking as yours, Sippy."

The Lord God hardened Pharaoh's heart indeed and he refused to let the people go. He kept grinding down on his teeth so much that his teeth got smaller and smaller. Then God came up with an unusual plague for the seventh, one that would come from the sky.

God spoke to Moses, "Tomorrow go to Pharaoh with Aaron. Warn him this time that if he does not free My people from bondage, My seventh plague is coming."

Moses asked Zipporah to wake him in case he slept too long. She asked, "What plague is God performing next?"

"I don't know but I'm sure it's a beaut."

Zipporah did awaken Moses before sunrise since he needed to wash, dress, pray, and eat a hearty breakfast. Moses strode on the balls of his feet alongside Aaron until they stood in front of Pharaoh when he was soaking in his tub trying to soothe the pain from the boils.

"What evil thing will you do now?" Pharaoh asked.

"If you let our people go, we won't have to do anything," Aaron said. "Just say the word and all the plagues will cease."

"Jump in the Nile next to a crocodile," Pharaoh said.

"You've asked for it," Aaron said. "We'll give you a day to change your mind, and if you remain stubborn, hail will fall from the sky tomorrow. The hail will be as large as oranges and any remaining animals or people who are outside will be killed."

"I don't believe that can happen," Pharaoh said. "I never saw hail bigger than grapes."

CHAPTER 16

THAT EVENING MOSES and Aaron and their wives sat around the kitchen table drinking milk and noshing on dates and figs. Zipporah said, "I wish that God wouldn't harden Pharaoh's heart so much. I love traveling. I'd like to leave for parts unknown with nothing to interrupt my plans."

Moses looked at his wife and said, "You know God moves in mysterious ways. We don't know the reason. It's possible we'll be traveling sooner than we think."

Elisheva, Aaron's wife, an obese and contrary older woman, said, "I know why God is sending so many plagues. He wants Pharaoh to suffer like he's made us suffer."

"I don't know about that," Aaron said. "We shouldn't try to understand God's methods. We're only humans with small brains, but God knows and sees everything. We need to be humble."

"I agree," Moses said. "Perhaps the hail will be the last plague, but who can say? Maybe God wants to send one hundred plagues."

"I hope not," Zipporah said. "That would take too long. Our people are writhing in pain. We need our suffering not to be prolonged."

Elisheva took out the pit from the date she had bitten into and placed it in the bowl that was getting filled up. It had a hill of pits. "I'm not so uncomfortable in Goshen. We have food and drink and I have two robes, one for every day and one for the Sabbath."

"What about our men who are suffering?" Zipporah asked, as she glared at Elisheva.

"That's not our fault," Elisheva said. "God shouldn't have caused them to suffer in the first place."

"Let's not argue," Aaron said, as he leaned over and placed his hand on his wife's shoulder. Aaron was a very compassionate peacemaker, and he had much practice for that at home. In fact, that's where his legendary capacities as a "lover and pursuer of peace" originated.

The next morning the Egyptians who believed that the Hebrew God was going to send hail moved their servants and cattle into the shelter of their houses. The other Egyptians who still thought that their Pharaoh was the main god left their cattle outside.

When Moses raised his staff to heaven, thunder roared and hail spread over the land. Fire broke out amidst the hail. The Egyptians fled for their lives. Man, beast, and herbs were smitten and cries of pain were heard everywhere except in the land of Goshen.

Once again Pharaoh sent for Moses and Aaron. "What do you have to say for yourself?" Aaron asked the king.

"I've sinned this time. Your Lord is righteous, and my people and I are wicked." Pharaoh's head hung low and he cast his eyes on the black marble floor. He looked like he really meant what he said. "I'll let you go now for I don't want any more mighty thunderings and grapefruit-sized hail."

"All right," Aaron said. "We'll ask the Lord God to stop the thunder and the hail. But make sure you don't change your mind."

"I won't," Pharaoh said. "I promise."

#

Pharaoh and Mrs. Pharaoh were in bed when Mrs. Pharaoh noticed that the thunder had stopped. There was no more pinging and banging of the hail. She turned to her husband. "It's all over. Even though the flax and the barley were smitten, the wheat and the rye have not matured so we have plenty of grain left to make rolls and rye bread. Therefore, go back on your promise and don't let those lazy Hebrews go."

"You are so wise, my dear. I'll never let them go."

#

Once again God spoke to Moses and told him to go to Pharaoh again, for He had hardened his heart in order to prove that His signs come from Him. "I want your children and grandchildren to know what I have done."

"What plague will you send, Lord?" Moses asked.

"I will send locusts."

Moses asked, "What will a few insects accomplish?"

"I will not send just a few," the Lord God said. "I will cover the land with so many locusts that everything that grows will be eaten."

"Good idea," Moses said. "The Egyptians will starve to death."

The next day Moses and his brother Aaron went to the palace. They had to wait until the Pharaoh emerged from his royal chamber to give him the news.

Pharaoh looked cross. He wrinkled his brow. "Look fellas, I've survived all your plagues up to now and if you have another one I'll live through that too. You don't scare me because I'm the main god here."

Aaron said, "We come to tell you about the next plague that will cover the whole of Egypt. God will send locusts."

"Locusts?" Pharaoh laughed. "Locusts don't bite like mosquitoes. I'm not afraid of locusts."

"You don't understand," Aaron said. "These locusts will eat every tree, every plant, everything that's growing. They'll fill your palace, your homes, the homes of your servants and guards, and the houses of all the Egyptians. Let my people go or you'll be sorry you didn't."

"Never," Pharaoh said. "I'll never let your people go."

Then Pharaoh's butler turned to him. "Free them, Majesty. They're a thorn in our bodies. What do we need them for? Their god is making us suffer."

Pharaoh's face turned the color of beets. "They don't have a god. It's all magic. They're skilled magicians. Don't be afraid of a few locusts. We'll kill them with fly swatters."

"I don't know about that," the butler said. "Locusts are too big for fly swatters."

"Fool," Pharaoh said. "We'll use big fly swatters."

"We don't have big fly swatters," the butler informed Pharaoh.

"Okay, send for the fakers again that I may speak with them."

That afternoon Moses and Aaron returned. Pharaoh and Mrs. Pharaoh were seated on their respective thrones. Mrs. Pharaoh had a cushion on hers because she had been having back trouble.

"All right, you two, I've changed my mind," Pharaoh said. "You can go. But who will go with you?"

Moses said, "We'll take our children, our senior citizens, our sons and our daughters. Furthermore, we'll take our flocks of sheep, our herds of cattle, and every single goat. We have to hold a feast unto the Lord God."

"Go only with your men," Pharaoh said. "Don't take all those other people and animals. I need them. Guards remove these two troublemakers from my presence."

After they had been taken out, the Lord spoke to Moses. "Take your staff and stretch it over the land of Egypt and the locusts will come and eat all the vegetation that is left." And Moses did as he was commanded.

#

Inside the house of Akh the Egyptian and his wife Dalilah, which means 'weak', Dalilah screamed bloody murder. The locusts were scattered all over her body. Even though Akh had the same number of locusts on him, he loved his wife and tried to remove them from her body by slapping her.

"You're hurting me worse than the locusts are," Dalilah cried as she spit a locust out of her mouth.

"I'll remove them one by one," Akh said. "But I can't move. I can't get a candle. I'm frozen in darkness. I would like to eat a loaf of rye bread but it's impossible. Maybe we should pray to the Hebrew god to remove this plague."

"I'm praying already," Dalilah said, as more locusts flew around her head.

In every Egyptian house the same scenario was taking place. The Lord brought an east wind all day and all night, and in the morning there were so many locusts that they blocked the light of the sun. The land was so dark it looked like a moonless night. The insects ate all the fruit of the trees and every herb. There was no green thing left in all of the land of Egypt, with the exception of Goshen where the Hebrews lived.

I bet you know what comes next. Yes, Pharaoh called in haste for Moses and Aaron. They took their time in arriving at the palace. Pharaoh delivered the very same speech he had given when the hail descended. It was boring, but Moses and Aaron gave him respect by listening to what he had to say, even though they well knew that he wasn't being truthful. Pharaoh said, "I'm a sinner. Forgive me. Please, please take the locusts away."

Moses again asked the Lord God to stop the plague, and the locusts died.

But God wasn't finished with the plagues and He said, "Stretch your hand towards heaven. I will bring extreme darkness." Moses did as he was commanded and a thick absence of light fell over Egypt day and night for three days' time. It was so dark that Akh and Dalilah couldn't see each other. The same held true in every Egyptian house.

The Lord God spoke to Moses again. "Go with your little ones only and sacrifice to Me."

Moses looked puzzled. "How can we sacrifice if we don't have our cattle?"

God said, "Then take your cattle with you."

"We shall do as You command," Moses said. It didn't take long for Moses to gather unblemished cows to sacrifice to the Lord God.

I'm sure you know what happened next. Pharaoh's heart hardened. He wouldn't let the Hebrews go to offer sacrifices. Pharaoh was a real mean dude. He said to Moses, "If I see you ever again, I'll have you killed."

Moses came up with a perfect answer. He said, "Pharaoh, you have spoken well. I'll make sure never ever to look upon your ugly face again." With that statement Moses raced from the throne room and returned to Goshen.

CHAPTER 17

FOR THE LORD there is no time as people know it. I, Methuselah, am an angel, and I can inform you on my authority that we also don't mark time in Heaven. What happened next was that God saw a beautiful temple erected for Him and that meant He needed to instruct the Hebrews to collect jewels of silver and gold that they could use for construction.

God told Moses, "I intend to bring the last plague to Egypt and afterwards Pharaoh will let you go."

"What is this plague?" Moses asked. *Will it be vicious beasts? Will it rain without stopping? Will the sun shine continuously twenty-four hours a day?*

God said, "At midnight all of the first-born Egyptians will die, even the first-born of the beasts."

I never considered that, Moses thought. *Pharaoh will suffer greatly when he loses his oldest son.*

"This month shall be the first month on your calendar," God said. "On the tenth day of this month every man shall take a male lamb without blemish, or a sheep or a goat. This animal they shall keep until the fourteenth day of the month, and they shall kill the animal in the evening."

"What time?" Moses asked.

"When the sun sets," God said. "They shall take the blood of the animal and put it on the upper doorpost of their homes.

Then they shall roast the animal and eat it with unleavened bread and bitter herbs."

"Please wait a minute, Lord God; I have to write this down."

"So be it," God said. "I will wait."

"Got it," Moses said, as he finished writing and put down his quill.

"I will continue," God said. "Anything that is left over they shall burn with fire. Tell them to keep their shoes on, dress with warm clothing, and eat in haste for it is the Lord's Passover. They will have to leave in a hurry. For I shall pass through the land of Egypt and I will smite all the first-born, man and beast. But my people with the blood on their doorposts in Goshen I will pass over."

"Wow!" Moses cried.

"Additionally," God said, "This day will be a memorial for future generations to keep. Seven days my people will eat unleavened bread. Their homes shall be cleaned until there isn't a crumb of leavened bread in them. And if this is not done, I shall cut off their souls from Israel."

"Oh my!" Moses said. *All the women will have to do a whole lot of cleaning. Every cabinet, closet, floor, clothes, pots, pans, dishes, and silver will have to be scrubbed like crazy. The women won't like this, but they'll have to do it.*

As Methuselah, I know what happens later. I see the future. The poor women work hard for many months before Passover. Most of their hands get sore, red, and blistered. Their backs ache, but they have no choice but to clean every corner of their houses or apartments or condos. The rich women and their husbands and kids go to kosher hotels where the management cleans. Some families go to their temples for *Seders* the first two nights of Passover and that saves the women some work. If they make Passover at home, they pay extra for special foods. There is a difference between some unleavened bread, called *matzos*, and others that are called crackers, and some people buy *matzos* that are as hard as cardboard. As far as flavor goes, if they add butter or jam it's acceptable, but don't ask what it does to the stomach.

Back to biblical times. Sure enough at midnight the Lord smote all the first-born in the land of Egypt. It was a blood bath. Pharaoh mourned like everyone else, but it was worse for him because his first-born was supposed to be the next Pharaoh. Also, his wife blamed him now for not giving in to Moses' demands although she had encouraged him earlier in his stubbornness. He wanted to pull out his hair, but his hair had been shaved off. Instead he beat his chest until it drew blood. The people came to the palace and rose up with a great cry, "Mighty Pharaoh, let the Hebrews go. Otherwise we'll revolt and let them go ourselves. Our children and beasts are dead and it's your fault."

Pharaoh dried his eyes and sent for Moses and Aaron. "Okay, all right, yes, I will let you and your people go. Get out of Egypt immediately, and do it fast."

"Can we take our flocks?" Moses asked.

"Yes, take anything you want but get out of here. When you worship your God, put in a good word for me too."

Moses said to Joshua, "Pharaoh said to take anything. Let's tell our people to 'borrow' the Egyptians' jewels of silver and gold, their clothes, pillows, quilts, and some rolls of papyrus."

You never saw such grabbing by the Hebrews. They took anything they could get their hands on. They took the pillow cases and stuffed them with what they thought they would need on the road to the Promised Land. They despoiled Egypt and Pharaoh was glad to get rid of them—until he changed his mind again.

When they couldn't carry anything else on their camels, donkeys, and on their backs, they left. The Bible says 600,000 men exited Egypt, but there couldn't have been that many. Remember I told you the scribe who wrote the Bible was dyslexic. I don't know the exact number but it's hard to believe there were 600,000 men, not counting the Levites, the women and the children—which if you figured it out would come to close to two million. The land couldn't have supported that many people.

Do you know who went with them? Egyptians, who were disenchanted with Pharaoh and the Egyptian belief in multiple gods, accompanied the Hebrews. The Bible calls them a 'mixed multitude'. It doesn't say anything about the Princess, but she rode on a camel in back of Moses and Zipporah. She loved her two adopted grandsons, and even though her father begged her to stay in Egypt, she refused and left Egypt with the Israelites.

CHAPTER 18

THE CHILDREN OF Israel rode on lumpy camels and bumpy donkeys, and those who didn't have beasts of burden walked and wore out their sandals. Then they walked barefoot. That was the start of the profession of podiatry.

After Pharaoh had a restless sleep, he realized the treasure he had lost. *All those slaves who were building my pyramids, my temples, my obelisks—gone. What have I done?* Then Pharaoh got out of bed, got dressed, had his breakfast, and called his chief security guard, Rho. "Get the best six hundred chariots ready with the best drivers and soldiers. We're going after the Hebrews to bring them back."

"What about the second-rate chariots?" Rho asked.

"Assemble every chariot, even the ones with defective wheels. We'll bring them back, and for their defiance they'll work even harder than ever before."

"Defective wheels?" Rho asked.

"They should've kept their chariots in good shape. I don't care if the drivers have accidents," Pharaoh said.

"Are you going to lead us?"

"You better believe it. I'm no coward. I'm the king of Egypt, the god of the Egyptians. Another thing I just remembered."

"Yes?"

"Have all the captains tell their troops to insert wax ear plugs in their ears. There's going to be a lot of noise."

"But, Your Majesty, with ear plugs in their ears blocking out sounds they won't hear any orders."

"Oooh! Never mind the ear plugs. I don't care if they lose their hearing as long as they bring back my slaves."

Pharaoh didn't know that the Lord God had hardened his heart when he stepped into his chariot, the one with the painted pictures of lions and tigers on it and spinning axle-knives. It was a chariot of wheeled death that also had a plush rug on the bottom for Pharaoh to stand on with his delicate royal feet.

The sound was deafening when they set out. The chariots with their horses racing at full speed kicked up so much dust the drivers couldn't see each other. There were so many accidents of chariots colliding that a large number of wheels fell off. By the time they reached the Children of Israel between Migdol and the sea they had lost 228 chariots.

When Pharaoh drew close, the Children of Israel saw them and they were very frightened. They cursed and grumbled to Moses, "Did you take us here to die in the wilderness? We were satisfied serving the Egyptians. Now look at us. What have you done?"

"Don't be scared," Moses said. "See the salvation of the Lord, for He shall fight for you."

"When will it be?"

Moses said in a strong voice, "Today."

"What time?"

"At dawn."

"Are you sure?" they asked.

"Not exactly, but close."

"We're still scared."

Then Moses reassured them with one word, "RELAX." Believe it or not, he remembered a lesson from his Anger Management class, though he had considered it a complete waste of time.

Moses heard the voice of the Lord, "Lift up your staff over the sea. The sea will divide. The Children of Israel will walk on dry ground. Tell your people to go forward. The Egyptians will follow and the sea walls will collapse over the chariots. The horsemen and the foot soldiers who have followed will drown."

God's angel, who had gone before the people in a pillar of cloud, withdrew behind them. Darkness fell upon the Egyptians and they remained where they were. Moses stretched out his hand and a strong east wind blew with a fury so that the Red Sea became two walls on either side of the dry bed for the people to walk through.

The next day at dawn the Children of Israel stood with wonder looking at the path that was to lead them to freedom. But the people were afraid to step into the dry land as they thought the sea might tumble back down to drown them. But Moses's sister Miriam marched right in. Tradition says it was Nachshon, but it was actually Miriam who went in ahead of him. Nachshon had guts too, but he got his courage from watching *her*. When nothing bad happened, the Children of Israel followed. It took almost all day for them to cross to the other side. Then the angel lifted the darkness from the eyes of the Egyptians. The sea became a sea again. The Egyptians perished in the water but Pharaoh turned around and didn't pursue them.

He returned to his palace and lived a long troubled life until he died at the age of ninety-two. He had three wives and was busy having children most of his life. The sons totaled 111 and it would have been one more if the tenth plague hadn't killed his first-born. He had fifty-one daughters and was burdened by having to order all those expensive robes to clothe them properly. Eventually he became manic- depressive and had to send for his masseur three times a day because in biblical times there weren't psychiatrists. One of his wives Isetnofret was so upset that all her male friends had drowned that she stopped talking for the rest of her life.

Pharaoh kept having nightmares about the time when his good chariots and a very large number of soldiers went deep into the dry bed of the Red Sea. The walls of the sea had collapsed on them. I, Methuselah, relate this part of the account with sorrow, when the Egyptians drowned, even the horses, with the exception of some chariots at the end of the column that were saved. The ones who survived had pleaded to Pharaoh, "Let us flee from the face of Israel. Their God fights for them."

"I guess we'd better," Pharaoh had said. "Let's get out of here."

The Children of Israel gathered around and saw what the Lord God had done to the Egyptians and their faith was renewed. One woman said, "They tried to conquer us. We won. Let's eat!"

When they finally settled in the Promised Land forty years later, one enterprising man manufactured T-shirts in different sizes that read "I CROSSED THE RED SEA."

When they traveled from Rameses to Succoth, they stopped off to bake unleavened cakes, *matzo*, and they complained bitterly about what the *matzo* was doing to their digestive systems. That was the first of the many complaints to come.

One of the young men said, "My stomach aches. I'm stuffed to the gills like a garbage pail."

"Don't eat so much *matzo*," his wife advised him. "Here are some prunes. I hope they'll help."

The Bible says that the Hebrews had dwelt in Egypt for 430 years, but the figure may not be accurate. My belief as Methuselah is that they dwelt there long after they should've gone to a better place. Even 210 years, as one scholar interprets, was too long. But of course people in captivity develop a "slave mentality" and accept the status quo. I do understand that.

God reiterated to Moses about who should attend the Passover service. He said, "All circumcised men, all circumcised servants, all women, and all children. Now I want you to sanctify to Me your first-born males and first-born animals."

"Yes, Lord God, we shall obey."

Moses instructed the people about everything that God had said. "The Lord God will bring us to the land of the Canaanite, the Hittite, the Amorite, the Hivite, and the Jebusite."

One father cried out, "If we go to all five countries, we'll be exhausted. Let's settle in one place where we can raise our children to worship God."

"It's not up to me," Moses said.

"Then who is it up to?" the man asked.

"The Lord God. I am only His messenger. He leads and we follow."

"Is there anything else we should be aware of?"

"Yes, there is. You must keep Passover and tell your children how the Lord brought us out of bondage from the land of Egypt. You must talk about all the plagues that were rained down on Pharaoh. That is very important."

When the Children of Israel were told at the last minute that the time had come for them to leave Egypt, they swiftly packed whatever was valuable to them. Miriam had a good friend by the name of Aviva. Miriam ran to Aviva's house and told her, "Don't leave your musical instruments behind. We'll need them. And at the crucial time when they gathered together after emerging from the Red Sea, Miriam and Aviva rounded up all the women.

Suddenly the men heard music from afar. It wasn't rock and roll. It had a different beat. Miriam and Aviva and all the women were singing songs of victory, dancing, and playing timbrels. A timbrel is a hoop of wood with parchment inside and bells all around. I, Methuselah, nowadays call it a tambourine. What singing, what dancing, and such carrying like you never saw in your life. Miriam sang the world's first hip-hop song and it went like this:

> To the Lord we sing
> Oh mighty King
> We have fled
> Across a dry bed
> On the sea
> To be free

Bells we ring
Dance and sing
Bow and nod
Giving thanks to God
For eliminating strife
Granting us long life.

CHAPTER 19

FOR SOME UNKNOWN reason, maybe it's in the DNA, the Children of Israel were always complainers. Nowadays they complain about the weather, the condition of the stock market, the state of the government, the high cost of membership in synagogues and temples, the naughty behavior of children, and the problems they have with in-laws. In biblical times not only weren't they grateful to Moses who led them out of bondage to freedom, but they voiced serious complaints that the Bible calls "murmuring." A lot of the time it was under their breath; more often than you would like to believe, however, you could hear it loud and clear.

Meyer was the ringleader when they spent three days in the wilderness of Shur. "Moses, the people are thirsty. Moses, there is no water in Shur."

Moses took this complaint seriously although it might not have sounded like he did. "Are you sure there is no water in Shur?"

"We're sure."

So Moses marched them to Marah, where they found water. You would surmise that they would be satisfied, but, no, they weren't. Meyer came to Moses and said, "This water is bitter. We can't drink it."

"Put in a teaspoon of sugar, or if you don't have sugar, try honey," Moses said, with a long face.

Meyer said, "I'm elected to talk for all the people. 'Marah' means 'bitter' and that's why they call this place by that name. No amount of honey can sweeten bitter water."

"I'll see what I can do," Moses said. He cried to the Lord God, "Please give my people sweet water."

God heard Moses and showed him a tree—a very, very small tree. Moses broke off a branch and threw it into the water and the water became sweet.

Do you think the people were grateful? They weren't. Meyer said, "There's not enough water."

"If you listen to God's commandments and not complain so much, He will give you more water."

Meyer said, "We'll try to do what's right. I'm not promising anything, but we'll attempt to do what God wants."

"Then let's move on," Moses said. The next morning the caravan moved more briskly than usual. They came to Elim on the fifteenth day of the second month after they left Egypt. Elim had an oasis and palm trees and a mild climate without mosquitoes. It was prime land. Were the children of Israel grateful? They were not. Even in modern times, I Methuselah, still hear how they complain—"Moses dragged us through the desert to the only land in the Middle East that didn't have oil."

The entire population of the Children of Israel complained loudly to Moses and Aaron, "In Egypt we had meat and plenty of bread, and you have brought us forth into this wilderness to starve us with hunger."

Moses called to the Lord God again for help, for he knew not what to do. "God, my people are hungry. Can you do something to calm their fraught nerves and fill their bellies, like sending us some rye bread or pumpernickel?"

God said, "I hear their cries. I have a solution. I will send down bread from heaven. Every day the people can collect it and eat. On the sixth day I will send double the amount from which they will be able to save half for the seventh day, which is the Sabbath."

Moses informed his people about the offering from heaven and about the sixth day's double supply. You would think that they'd be happy with the news, but they complained once again. Meyer, their leader, said, "What about meat? We're used to eating meat?"

Moses said, "You'll get your meat. I hope you like quail, for many quail will fly overhead and you'll be able to shoot them down. Now stop complaining because I can't take it anymore."

Then a group of men and women sat around the fire complaining like crazy. Lela said, "He rushed us out of the house so fast I didn't have time to take my best bowl."

Stu, the oldest man there, said with a whistle in his voice, "You think that's such a tragedy? I left behind my false teeth. How am I going to chew on a quail?"

Meyer came along and was annoyed by that complaint. "Stu," he said, "If you don't stop putting your foot in your mouth, you'll get athlete's foot."

After he left, Selma said, "I rushed out without my best robe."

Tessie said, "I'm freezing. I didn't take my hand-sewn blanket."

Mike looked them all over, "I left all my soap in my house. I can't bathe."

Then Lela, Stu, Selma, and Tessie smelled Mike's foul odor. All got up and left Mike by himself.

The next morning the Children of Israel saw spread out all over the earth lacy dew that evaporated and left something that looked like crackers. "What's that?" Selma asked Moses.

"This is the bread that the Lord is giving you to eat. It's called '*manna*'. You'll love it for breakfast, and for dinner you can eat quail. You'll dine like royalty."

"How much should I take?" Selma asked.

"You may have an *omer*?"

"What's an '*omer*'?"

"It's about a little more than nine cups."

Selma frowned. "I left my house so fast I left all my gorgeous cups behind."

Moses said, "Take as much as will satisfy your hunger. Your husband probably will gather more for he's a hefty man." *He's really very fat, but I didn't want to say that and hurt her feelings.*

Selma said, "I have an aching back. I can't bend down and pick up the food."

"Have your husband do that for you," Moses said.

"You don't know my husband."

"Then ask your children."

"My children? You think my dozen children will help me? They would rather play games than help their mother."

"Do you have any friends?" Moses asked.

"You think I have time for friends? Taking care of twelve children, feeding my husband, doing laundry, and cleaning the house have left me no time for friends."

EXODUS ACCORDING TO METHUSELAH

Miriam overheard this conversation. "I'll gather the manna for you."

"I can't trouble you for that. You're an old lady," Selma said with compassion.

"I may be old, but I'm as strong as an ox," Miriam said.

Tessie came along and butted in. "I don't like grains. Can't we have eggs for breakfast?"

"No," Moses said. "Manna is tasty. It's like crackers sweetened with honey."

"I'm on a diet," Tessie said. "Honey is fattening. How about oatmeal? Can we get oatmeal?"

"No there isn't any," Moses said, as his face reddened with anger. These complainers were beginning to get to him. "And I want you to remember not to leave anything over. Finish eating whatever you gather."

Do you think that Tessie obeyed what Moses had said? She did not. She left two cups of manna over and the next morning they had a disgusting odor and worms squirming all around in it. Moses became even more enraged. The Anger Management classes he had taken in Egypt had not done him that much good.

"Now Tessie," Moses said, "I'm telling everyone to gather twice as much manna tomorrow which is the sixth day and to rest on the Sabbath so that you won't have to work on the Sabbath."

Some of the Hebrews were so stubborn and lazy that they didn't gather twice as much. On the Sabbath they went into the field and behold there wasn't any manna. The Lord said to Moses, "How long is it going to take before my commandments and laws are followed?"

And Moses said to Aaron, "Put an *omer* full of manna in a pot and lay it before the Lord God as a sacrifice." *My people should be grateful that they have food to eat and water to drink.* "I think we better get moving and give the people something to keep them occupied. They're concentrating on food too much."

The people packed their belongings and started on another journey from the Wilderness of Sin. When they stopped to rest and relieve themselves, Tessie approached Moses. "I have nothing with which to wipe myself," she complained bitterly.

Moses recalled how when he was in the palace he used linen wipes. All royalty and nobles were given piles of linen wipes every week. The only material they had taken with them was the papyrus that grew up to fifteen feet on the banks of the Nile River. The Egyptians had used it for writing. Moses turned to Tessie, "Give me some time and I'll come up with a solution."

Taking the papyrus, Moses smashed the stalks. He cut them, soaked them, flattened them, and dried them. They dried quickly in the desert sun. Then Moses cut them into small squares and handed them to Tessie, who with little appreciation and no words of gratitude offered a weak smile. People think that toilet paper hadn't been invented until the nineteenth century, but Moses was the very first person who came up with the idea in the midst of the sandy desert. Even the ancient Greeks didn't use paper. They managed with clay and stone. The Romans used sponges and salt water. I, Methuselah, give Moses the true credit for his invention. Nowadays the United States spends more than $6 billion a year on toilet tissue, more than any other nation in the world and that's how important toilet tissue is. I'm therefore saying that of all Moses' inventions toilet paper was not the least important.

The next day the Israelites journeyed on. It was a long time before they stopped and pitched their tents, but they finally did in a place called Rephidim. The trip was most draining. They dropped to the ground fatigued. The sun shone with such a high intensity that the Children of Israel got severely sunburned. They sweated gallons. When they craved the relief of cool water in their mouths and throats, there was none.

One of the younger single men by the name of Hiram meaning "exalted brother" was interested in getting married. He didn't like his last name, which was Hur. Since he had been a child, kids teased him saying, "Hiram Hur is a her, not a him." His wife would need to take his name and he wondered if a pretty maiden by the name of Hannah, meaning "gracious," would accept the name "Hannah Hur." Points in his favor were that he was muscular, strong, and loyal to Moses.

Thousands of men and women cried out to Moses, "We need water. There is water, water everywhere but not a drop to drink. Why did you bring us here? We were better off in Egypt where there was plenty of water from the Nile River. Some leader you are! You have deceived us."

However both Hannah and Hiram were devoted to Moses and they didn't join the complainers. They listened with close attention to Moses' answer. With annoyance in his voice Moses said, "Why do you always find fault with me? I'm trying my best. Why do you tempt the Lord?"

The people shook their fists as they answered, "You brought us out of Egypt, a civilized country with buildings and art, all kinds of real roast beef and wine, and now your goal is to get rid of us. We don't trust you. You're killing the adults, the children, and our cattle with thirst." They searched on the ground for stones, picked some up, and hurled the stones at Moses who cried, "*Oy vey!*"

Moses turned once again to the Lord God. "What shall I do with these people? They are the worst complainers in the history of the world? They have collected stones and are ready to throw them at me. In fact one man threw a stone at me that hit my ankle. Zipporah had to bandage it. This isn't the way I'd like to die."

"Be brave, Moses," God said. "Take your staff and go to the rock that is in Horeb. Smite it and you will see that water will flow out of it. The people will be able to quench their thirst. They will drop their stones and all will be well."

Moses did as he was told and it did come to pass that there was enough water. Moses named the place 'Massah', which means "testing," for his temper was surely tested, and he also called it 'Meribah' which means "quarreling." That was an obvious name.

Hiram ran to collect water for Hannah. He brought it over to where she was sitting on the ground fanning herself, suffering from intense thirst. "Here," he said, "I brought you a jug of water and a cup to put it in. Let me put it to your lips." Hiram bent down and helped Hannah take a sip.

Hannah looked at Hiram's face. His lips were parched. "Thank you. You're most kind. Have you had any water yourself yet?"

"I'll get some later," he said.

"Take some of mine," Hannah said, as she noticed his muscular arms.

"Thank you. Any time you need help with anything, don't hesitate to call me. My name is Hiram Hur, spelled '**HUR**.'"

"What a nice name," Hannah said with a big smile.

They got married in a month. That was the beginning of a lifelong romance. As fortunate husbands in such happy marriages would later say, "My wife is not only my wife, she's my best friend."

CHAPTER 20

THE AMALEKITES HAD nothing to do with kites. Spears—yes! Bows and arrows—yes! They were a rough and tumble people who were descended from one of Esau's clans. Jacob had stolen the patriarchal blessing from Esau when Esau was desperate for food, and it seems that this clan of Esau never forgave Jacob and his descendants for that. They had a really mean streak and had it in for the Children of Israel even though they weren't camped in their territory, just resting nearby in Rephidim. The Hebrews had no intention of invading their land and the Amalekites knew it. But they decided that since they were in the area they were going after them.

Their chief was named Bull and when he spoke he sounded like a bullhorn. Early in the morning he gathered his army together. He talked to the captains of each squad. "The Israelites intend to invade our fertile land. They're close by and they're a serious threat to us. Therefore, arm yourselves and we will destroy every last one of them."

Captain Dragon spoke up, "When will we strike?"

Chief Bull said in a thunderous voice, "Tomorrow one hour before sunrise."

"What time is that?" Captain Dragon dared to ask.

"Figure it out for yourself," Chief Bull said and strode away.

The following day the Children of Israel, who weren't prepared for war as they never had been in one, suffered losses before the Amalekites withdrew.

Moses met with Joshua after the battle. "I want you to select strong men to fight the Amalekites. I'll stand on that small mountain close by and hold up my staff to heaven and we'll defeat our treacherous enemy."

Aaron spoke to his wife in their tent. "Now, now dear, no tears. The Lord God will protect us. He didn't bring us out of Egypt to get killed."

She dried her tears with an edge from the bottom of her worn robe. "I'm afraid that you'll get killed if you volunteer to fight."

"I have a strange feeling that I won't be a warrior, but that there is another task that God has set for me to perform."

"You need strength to do that task," she said. "Here is a plate of manna and a cup of water. If you're still hungry, I'll collect some more manna. There's more on the ground."

Moses told his sister Miriam that he intended to climb the small mountain so he could be closer to God.

"God is everywhere," Miriam said, "and you're an old man. An old man shouldn't be climbing mountains."

"I may be old, but I can still climb. I'll use my staff for a cane, and it will help me make it to the top. Actually I made a mistake in calling it a small mountain. It's just a hill."

"Hill shmill, it doesn't make any difference. Stay on the ground and wait for God to come to you like He's done before."

"You know, Miriam, you can be very stubborn."

"Me? Stubborn? What about you, Moses?"

When the Amalekites came with their troops the next morning, Joshua was ready with his newly formed army.

They engaged the Amalekites with an unbelievable fierceness. Aaron and Hur—not her, him—accompanied Moses to the top of the hill. Even though Moses used his staff getting there, he had to admit he was exhausted by the climb.

Moses noticed that when he held up both arms, the Israelites prevailed, but when he lowered them, Amalek prevailed. All this time Moses had been standing. "My arches have flattened," he said to Aaron and Hur. Nowadays people with flat feet have orthotics made for them, but they didn't have them in biblical times.

Aaron saw a flat rock close by. He led Moses to it and said, "Sit down my brother and rest."

Moses had hemorrhoids and he was very uncomfortable sitting on a hard rock. Aaron looked in his sack and took out a pillow. "Here sit on this. It has feathers inside and you'll be better able to sit more comfortably."

"Thank you," Moses said, as he sat down on the feathered pillow.

After a half-hour Moses couldn't hold his hands up any longer. "My arms hurt," he said.

Aaron turned to Hur. "What shall we do? When my brother lowers his arms, more of our soldiers get killed. This is a serious situation."

Hur bit down on his lips. "I have the answer. You stand on Moses' right side. I'll stand on his left side. We'll hold his arms up."

"What?" Moses cried. "You're going to hold my arms up? I never heard of such a thing. Do you think it will work? My arms will become numb and this technique will be ineffective."

EXODUS ACCORDING TO METHUSELAH

"Don't worry. Be happy," Aaron said. "This is a great solution. Now raise your arms up and we'll support them."

All day long until sunset, the two men on the hill were successful in raising Moses' arms. The Children of Israel drove the Amalekites away. Point of fact the Amalekites fled like a cyclone pursued them.

Then the Lord God said to Moses, "Write this for a memorial in a book. Eventually I shall utterly blot out the remembrance of Amalek from under heaven. Build me an altar."

Moses did build an altar and called the altar *"Adonai-nissi"* meaning "the Lord is my banner" since the Lord swore that He will wage war on Amalek from generation to generation.

I, Methuselah, have related how when I wasn't an angel and had been living on earth for 969 years, I married thirteen times. Some of my in-laws were dolls but there were others who I could have done without.

Moses did have one in-law who gave him a hard time—it was his critical mother-in-law who kept reminding him how he should have remained a prince in Egypt. He was lucky that his father-in-law Jethro, who happened to be a priest in Midian, was a compassionate man who looked out for his son-in-law. He helped Moses financially and with clever advice. When Moses had brought Israel out of Egypt, Jethro welcomed his daughter Zipporah and his grandsons Gershom and Eliezer into his home.

There came a time when Moses was encamped in the wilderness that Jethro brought him his wife and sons. Jethro's wife had objected bitterly saying, "Leave them with us. I need to see my grandsons grow up and I need Zipporah to do the cooking."

For once Jethro didn't listen to his wife. Moses and Jethro hugged and kissed each other when they met. There also was a lot of kissing going on among Moses, Zipporah, and their sons Gershom and Eliezer.

"How are you?" Jethro asked Moses.

"Not so good," Moses said.

"What's wrong?"

"Do you really want to know?"

"Sure. Tell me everything. Maybe I can be of help."

They went into Moses' tent and began a long conversation. Moses didn't hold anything back. He trusted Jethro to be discreet. He spoke about how the good Lord had brought ten plagues upon the Egyptians, and how hard-hearted Pharaoh was until God killed his first-born son. He continued telling about the times that the Children of Israel complained about the conditions in the wilderness. He showed Jethro the bandage on his leg where he had been hit by a stone.

Jethro listened quietly with sad eyes. *My poor son-in-law has suffered greatly. I must help him. I believe that his God is the true God and I bless Him.* When Moses stopped talking and fell asleep from exhaustion, Jethro took a burnt offering and offered sacrifices to the Lord.

Aaron and Joshua and Hur and their wives came and met Moses' family. After they had a feast, they thanked God for their deliverance.

The next morning a queue of one hundred Hebrew men stood outside Moses' tent. Hur—not her but him—to be fair to each had given them numbers from one to one hundred. Moses hurriedly ate his breakfast, sat outside on his chair, which had a pillow, and spoke to each man in turn.

"Number one," Moses called.

A man with a dark beard shaped like an isosceles triangle came forward. "My son refuses to help me get dressed. What should I do?"

Moses saw that the man was in his forties. "Why can't you dress yourself?"

The bearded man said, "My shoulders hurt and I need help."

"My advice to you is," Moses said, "have your son massage your shoulders. When you'll feel better, you'll be able to dress yourself. Number two."

The second in line came forward, "My wife insults me. I don't know how to respond."

Moses said, "What does she say?"

The man replied, "She calls me 'a lazy bum'."

Moses nodded. "Do you have any idea why?"

The man's face reddened. "Yes, I don't help her diaper my baby triplets."

Moses said, "Start helping her with the babies and she'll stop calling you names."

Jethro was standing nearby when he heard Moses—from sunrise to sunset—give his advice to all the people who showed up.

Inside the tent Jethro said to Moses, "Hearken to what I'm advising you, for it's good counsel. Pick God-fearing men who have common sense and teach them ordinances and laws. Select some to be chieftains of thousands, chieftains of hundreds, chieftains of fifties, and chieftains of tens. Let them judge the people."

"Then what will I be doing?" Moses asked.

"You judge great matters, but the others can judge small matters. What do you think?"

"I think that's a brilliant idea. I wonder why I hadn't thought of that myself?"

Jethro said, "You would have thought of it in due time, but you are too overloaded now to think straight. Remember to pick men who you can trust, who are God-fearing Israelites."

"I'll start immediately."

"Just a second," Jethro said. "It's midnight. Go to sleep. You'll have time to do this in the morning."

"Again you're right. I'm so glad you're my father-in-law, not only a father-in-law, but a very dear friend. I wish you could stay with us."

"I have to return to my own land. Meanwhile I'm glad you like my idea. If you need any more ideas, I'll be here for another week, but then, trust me, I have to go home. My wife expects me to take out the garbage. She never takes it out herself. The garbage by now must be as high as a mountain."

"All right, if you must go; but my intuition tells me that we'll meet again."

Jethro bit down on his lips as he tried not to let his eyes tear. "We must meet again. I'm glad that Zipporah married you, and I'm proud of you, Moses. Your name will go down in history and no one will remember who I am."

"Don't be so sure of that. You'll be remembered, on the contrary, for starting the judicial system. And if I know anything about the Children of Israel, they're gonna need good laws, not to speak of good judges."

CHAPTER 21

THREE MONTHS AFTER the Children of Israel left Egypt they departed from Rephidim. This time Moses was delighted that his wife and sons were with him. The entire caravan moved slowly in the wilderness because there weren't facilities there like rest stops and McDonalds.

Moses dismounted from his camel when they came to a mountain. The scenery was harsh. The mountain was barren, sandy and rocky with no vegetation, not even a tree. It had deep, dry ravines. Moses announced, "This is where we'll stay."

"How long will we be here?" his son Gershom asked.

"As long as it takes," Moses answered. "Now help me pitch the tent for our family."

Gershom answered, "Not only will I pitch the tent, but I'll help bring in supplies, and I'll gather the manna."

Moses held up his hand in an effort to stop his son from taking on too much. He said, "Multitasking is bungling up several things at once." That was the first time in the history of the world that the word 'multitasking' was used.

Once the tent was set up Moses heard God call to him, "Moses, Moses!"

Moses left the tent in an effort to have privacy for receiving God's message. He answered, "Here am I, your servant."

He heard God's voice call once again from the mountain. "Climb my mountain on the third day and I shall talk to you at the summit."

Meanwhile Gershom was collecting stones to place in a circle for an outdoor barbeque. All the able Hebrew men were doing the same, pitching tents, arranging rocks in circles for fire pits. Eliezer lit a fire. It took a while as he had no matches and he had to rub sticks together. Zipporah put a quail in the family's fire pit to roast for supper. Thousands of people were doing the same. The women did most of the cooking. They had brought some spices from Egypt when they fled the land of their enslavement. The pleasant aroma of roasted quail was in the air, no marshmallows, but plenty of meat. Families gathered together around the fire pits including Hannah and Hiram Hur. As far as the eye could see there were makeshift tents for sleeping. They didn't have electricity or bathrooms, but they managed.

There were no dishes to wash. Since Moses wasn't keen on washing dishes, he was content. They ate the roasted quail with their fingers and when they were finished, they licked their fingers clean, and then gave thanks to the Lord God.

Moses spoke privately to his wife, "God wants me to climb the mountain."

Zipporah frowned. "He should realize that you're an old man of eighty with arthritic bones and flat feet. Tell God that he can talk to you at the foot of the mountain."

"I can't do that. I have to obey His command."

Zipporah pursed her lips. "Then have Gershom and Eliezer help you climb up. Do you know that 4,200 cubits is very high?"

"I'll walk slowly. I can't take the boys with me. God wants to talk to me alone."

Zipporah bit down on her lips. "Then take your strongest staff, some dried meat, and a jug of water."

"All right, I'll take my staff, but I don't need food and water."

"You don't know how long you'll be up there. You'll die of hunger and thirst. I'm your wife. Listen to me. I only want you to come back healthy and strong. God asks you to do difficult things," Zipporah said, as she began to walk back to the tent.

"Don't worry so much. I'll be all right. God is protecting me. He's not asking me to climb a mountain and starve up there. He has an important reason that I'll find out about soon enough."

God spoke to Moses once again, "Speak to the Children of Israel and remind them how I bore them on wings of eagles from Egypt to this wilderness. They shall be a treasure to Me, a holy nation and a kingdom of priests."

Moses called the elders to him and repeated the Lord God's words. "Will you behave yourselves while I'm away?" he asked, still unsure about his complaining people's devotion to God.

The elders looked at each other and then turned to their leader, "All that the Lord hath spoken we will do."

Moses felt a wave of relief move through his body. He repeated to the Lord what the elders had said.

"Whenever I speak to you," the Lord said, "I will come in a thick cloud."

"I understand," Moses said. He approached the people and related to them what the Lord had said to him. He added, "I'll be giving you any new information that I'll receive from the cloud."

The Lord said, "Tell the people to sanctify themselves today and tomorrow by washing their clothes. The men shall separate themselves from the women."

Hannah Hur, who was standing amidst one group said, "How do I know that there will be enough water to wash everyone's clothes for two days in a row. There's a ton of laundry."

Moses answered patiently, "I shall ask The Lord God about the water."

Then he said to God who was in the thick cloud, "Almighty God, someone wants to know if there will be enough water to wash all the clothes twice."

God answered, "Tell Hur's wife not to worry. I will send plenty of water. I will be on Mount Sinai in the presence of all the people. Tell them to take heed that they not climb it or even touch the border, for if they do they shall die, man or beast. When the trumpet sounds on the third day, they will approach with clean clothes, men separated from women. Moses, tell them everything I just said at least three times for the people are quick to forget."

"Lord, I have trouble speaking, especially such a long speech three times. Is it all right for Aaron to speak for me?"

God answered, "I shall make your speech perfect, no hesitations or mispronunciations, and you shall deliver it in a powerful piercing voice."

CHAPTER 22

AND IT CAME to pass on the third day thunder roared and lightning zig-zagged across the sky. A loud trumpet sounded as a thick cloud settled upon the top of Mount Sinai. In the huge camp thousands upon thousands of the children of Israel trembled.

Hannah Hur wondered if she should have washed their clothes more than twice. Maybe the clothes needed three washes. She looked up and saw the top of the mountain smoking. She thought *God has come with fire.* She cast her eyes down to her bare feet and felt quaking under them.

A trumpet played one note louder and louder. Moses took his staff and began to climb the mountain. It didn't look to Hannah from the bottom as if he had any trouble stepping over rocks. He took every step like a strong young man. "Keep coming up," the Lord called down to him.

When Moses reached the summit, he was surprised to hear the Lord say, "Now go down and tell the people not to gaze up for if they do they will perish. Tell the priests to sanctify themselves and let them put boundaries around my mountain."

I'm getting a lot of exercise for a man my age, Moses thought, as he walked down. *It's easier to walk down than up. But I'll have to go up again. I hope God will give me time to relax Even if He won't, whatever He says I'll do.*

Moses made it up to the top a second time without any trouble, for God had given him enough strength to do it. So much adrenaline had poured into him that he didn't even need to rest. Moses took a very deep breath at the top of the mount and heard the voice of the Lord.

The Ten Commandments were longer at this momentous time, but I, Methuselah am shortening them for readers for the sake of brevity.

THOU SHALT HAVE NO OTHER gods BEFORE ME.
THOU SHALT NOT MAKE ANY GRAVEN IMAGES.
THOU SHALT NOT TAKE THE NAME OF THE LORD IN VAIN.
REMEMBER THE SABBATH DAY.
HONOR THY FATHER AND THY MOTHER.
THOU SHALT NOT KILL.
THOU SHALT NOT COMMIT ADULTERY.
THOU SHALT NOT STEAL.
THOU SHALT NOT BEAR FALSE WITNESS.
THOU SHALT NOT COVET.

Moses was the first person in history downloading a tablet from the Cloud. In his case, he had two tablets.

The people below saw the lightning and heard the blast of thunder and the loud noise of the trumpet. Hannah closed her eyes and put her fingers in her ears. She was with child and very sensitive to the din. She and Hiram and the others who were closer to the mountain moved back two hundred cubits and stood far off.

On the summit of Mount Sinai God spoke again to Moses, "Tell the children of Israel that I have spoken to you from Heaven. Make sure you say that they should not make gods of silver or gold. Make an altar and sacrifice burnt-offerings and peace-offerings to me of sheep and oxen. Then I shall bless you and them."

"From what should I make the altar?" Moses asked.

"Make it of untouched stone, not of stone that has already been hewn for if it is hewn, it is unacceptable."

God wrote the Ten Commandments on two stone tablets and they could be seen miraculously on the front and the back. "Take this to the Children of Israel," the Lord said.

Moses thought *I can't lift a full grown sheep. How am I going to carry these tablets down a rocky mountain?*

"Before you go down," God said, "I shall give you more laws that I shall not write on stone."

I'm eighty years old. How will I remember all these laws?

"You will stay up here for forty days and forty nights and I will increase your memory," God said.

Forty days and forty nights? I'll starve to death.

"You will not starve. I will enhance your physical capacities. Do not forget I created them in the first place."

But I need to sleep. And it's cold up here.

"Strengthen your resolve and your faith in Me, Moses. You will be able to go without sleep and you will not feel heat or cold."

The Lord God is reading my mind. I better keep it pure. Since God made the miracles of the plagues and parted the Sea of

Reeds, then God can keep me alive for forty days and forty nights without sleep, without food or water, or without feeling heat or cold. God bless God.

"Thank you, Moses! I can also read your mind, you know."

CHAPTER 23

GOD NEEDED MOSES to remain on Mount Sinai for a period of forty days since He had a bunch of rules and regulations he had to give to Moses for him to relate to the Children of Israel.

In biblical times there were times poor men became slaves, but they were called "servants" which sounds more respectable. Seymour was such a person. He had worked for the Hur family for six years and had married before that time and had fraternal twins, one son and one daughter. The law that God passed said that Seymour was to be set free in the seventh year and be allowed to leave with his family. If such a procedure had been followed in the nineteenth century, it would've prevented the Civil War or "The War Between the States" as Southerners call it.

God went even further. He said that if Seymour was given a wife by his master and she had children then he could leave by himself—but and this was a big "but"—if Seymour indicated that he loved his wife and children, then his master should bring him to the judges, and when the judges would rule he can stay, then the master should bring him to his house in front of the door post. The master should pierce his ear with an awl and he would continue being a servant.

Moses had a question. Something about an awl and a doorpost was bothering him. "Lord God what is an 'awl'?"

"An awl is a pointed instrument for piercing holes."

"Uh, oh!" Moses said. "That will surely hurt the slave."

"No," God said. "The end of the awl will be as small as a needle."

"I see," Moses said. "If the master puts holes in both of the slave's ears, then the slave can then wear earrings."

"No," God said. "That is not the purpose. One ear is enough, for an ear is the organ of hearing. Thus the piercing signifies the servant's promise of obedience. He is to realize that for the rest of his life he has to remain with the master."

"Ah ha!" Moses said. "But I don't understand why it has to be at a door. Couldn't it be done at a table?"

"No," God said. "A door symbolizes movement from one environment to another. The slave is not leaving, but moving permanently into his master's house."

"That makes sense," Moses agreed.

"Let us continue. If a father sells his daughter to be a maid-servant, and she does not please her master who wants her as a wife, then she shall go free."

"Yes," Moses said. "That is very fair."

"Also if the master has betrothed her to his son, she should be free to make up her own mind. And if the master marries again, she should have full rights as a wife."

"What are the full rights?" Moses asked.

"He should give her clothing, food, and the duty of marriage. And if he does not do this, then the maiden shall go free without him having to pay her money."

"But suppose she needs money to live on?" Moses asked.

"Her family will care for her."

"All right, I'm ready for the next law."

"If a man kills another man with premeditation, then he shall die, but if it is accidental then the victim shall flee to a special place."

God asked Moses, "Are you listening and memorizing what I am telling you?"

"Yes, my Lord God. I'm paying close attention."

"If a man kills his neighbor with intent, then he shall die."

"I agree," Moses said.

"Also if a man kills his father or his mother, he shall be put to death."

Moses nodded. "Nobody should kill his parents."

"If a man steals a person and sells him, he shall die."

"That makes sense."

"Also," God said, "If a person curses his father or mother, he shall be put to death."

Moses was puzzled. *Cursing is just using words. Why does God say this?*

"I can read your mind, Moses. Parents should be careful in training their children to be respectful to them. Yocheved and the Princess taught you respect. Cursing is cutting with the tongue. Parents stand in place of Me."

"I understand," Moses said. "Because of this ruling no child will ever curse his parents."

"That is what I hope for. And if a man strikes another and the other man does not die, the striker shall pay the victim for the loss of his time and shall pay the doctor's bills."

"What about boxing?"

"My law doesn't apply to recreational boxing."

"Okay."

"If a man strikes his male or female servant and the person dies right away, then he shall be punished. But if he or she lives a day or two, then he shall not be punished."

"Lord God, why is that?"

"There is a difference in the severity of the blow. If they die immediately, the man has been cruel, but if they do not suffer as much and if it is because he has upbraided them for an offense, he shall not be punished."

"God, did you just sneeze?"

"No, the sound you heard was lightning."

"That's good, because it wouldn't sound exactly right for me to say 'God bless you.'"

"There is a related law concerning a pregnant woman. If a man hurts her and she loses her child, the woman's husband shall punish him. The judges will decide how much he has to pay. Now the next part is misunderstood—for when I say 'an eye for an eye, a tooth for a tooth, a hand for a hand, and a foot for a foot, burning for burning, wound for wound, stripe for stripe' I really mean it figuratively, not literally."

"Lord God, it's very poetic. I really like your choice of words."

"I will continue. If a man smites the eye of his servant or the eye of his maid-servant, he shall let them go free. The same thing holds for a tooth."

"Only one tooth, Lord God?"

"Yes, even for just one tooth, for all teeth are necessary for eating and for beauty."

"That is why I brush my teeth every day," Moses remarked in a tired voice.

Hearing how Moses sounded, God said, "It appears like you need a break. Let us take one."

After the break Moses began to ponder about how future generations will apply all these laws.

God read Moses' mind and said, "Future generations will study my laws. Here is another one. If an ox gores a man or woman one time and they die, the ox shall be killed and the owner shall not be punished. But if the ox does this repeatedly, then both the owner and the ox shall be killed."

Moses thought about this and came up with another example. "Suppose the ox pushes a man-servant or a maid-servant, what should the judgment be?"

"'Killed' does not mean 'pushes'. In that case the ox shall be stoned and the master shall be awarded thirty shekels of silver."

Moses asked, "How many more judgments about oxen do You have?"

"Patience, Moses. There are only three more that have to do with an ox."

Moses' mind began to wander:

> There once was a very hungry ox
> That ate a few bagels with lox
> It stopped eating hay
> And the very next day
> Was buried in a big pine box.

Nowadays people aren't aware that it was Moses who created the first limerick. A limerick is a silly poem of five lines that is believed to have been popularized by Edward Lear, the author in 1846 in *The Book of Nonsense*; but I, Methuselah, know that it was Moses who first composed limericks.

Of course God was annoyed when Moses stopped concentrating. "Pay attention to My laws, Moses. You have to repeat them to the Children of Israel."

"I'm sorry, Lord God, my mind wandered. I've no excuse for such bad behavior except that the material really is a little difficult."

I, Methuselah, agree with Moses that the laws are difficult to understand. There are many more laws pertaining to oxen. I don't want to bore readers so I'll omit the rest of the laws. You are free to look them up and study them if you are so inclined.

Moses mind wandered. He thought, *I wonder what's happening at the base of this mountain. Is everything okay?*

God said, "Pay attention, Moses. Do not worry about the Children of Israel at the base of My mountain."

I, Methuselah, know that in 1922 a famous book of etiquette was published. Emily Post had written *Etiquette—The Blue Book of Social Usage*. It's a definitive guide for manners. The book was reported to be second only to the Bible because it has been the book which has been most often stolen from libraries. The principles of etiquette are consideration, respect, and honesty. God's laws, to be sure, are the basis for Emily Post's principles.

The Lord God went on and on stipulating more laws which I, Methuselah, say you can read for yourself. When the Lord God was finished he gave Moses the Ten Commandments written on two tablets of stone. But I want to move on to another section of the Bible.

CHAPTER 24

MEANWHILE "DOWN AT the ranch" people nowadays say; but I will say, more specifically, 'meanwhile down at the base of Mount Sinai' all kinds of happenings were taking place.

Two women, Chava and Yael, were talking loudly outside their tent. Yael said, "Moses has been up there for thirty days without food and water."

Chava groaned. "He must be dead."

The two women began to wail. Tears flowed down their faces. More women and men in nearby tents, and men also, came to see what the crying was all about.

Yael blew her nose. "We think Moses is dead. We haven't seen him for thirty days. Woe unto us."

An older woman by the name of Alte said, "Let's talk to Aaron. Maybe he can make us a god to worship."

Hundreds of people stood outside of Aaron's tent until he emerged. Another woman, Simchah, said, "We don't know what has happened to Moses. We need to pray to a god. Help us make a god."

Aaron didn't know what to do. He knew that Moses was in good shape since God was protecting him, but this crowd demanded he make a false god for them. To pacify them Aaron said, "Bring me your gold earrings and anything made of gold and I shall make you a golden calf."

It took Aaron ten days to make the golden calf and all that time he suffered with a migraine headache caused by a guilty conscience. When the calf was finished, some of the people—by no means all of the people—danced and sang around the calf while Aaron, his wife and sons, stood back frowning with displeasure. Mr. and Mrs. Hur joined them, but they could do nothing to stop the people who prayed to the idol.

When God sent Moses back down the mountain, He said, "Your stiff-necked people who you took out of Egypt have corrupted themselves. My wrath waxes hot against them."

When God used the word 'stiff-necked' He didn't mean they suffered from stiff necks. He meant they were stubborn.

"If you destroy them, what will the Egyptians say?" Moses asked. "Remember Abraham, Isaac, and Jacob. You told them that You would multiply their seed. Please don't destroy my stiff-necked people."

The Lord God listened to Moses and He repented of the evil which he thought to do unto His people.

After descending the mountain, Moses came to the camp and saw the people worshipping the idol. Even though he had taken the Anger Management class twice, he became enraged and cast the two tablets on the ground. They shattered into many pieces. Then he took the calf, burned it in the fire, and ground it to powder. He put the powder in jugs of water and made the Children of Israel drink it. Yael made a face as she took a sip.

Moses said, "Drink every last drop."

Yael did. "My stomach hurts," she complained.

"Drink!" Moses commanded. After all the others had drunk the gold water and grumbled about their pain, Moses didn't feel sorry for any of them.

Moses kept fuming. Ranting and raging he said to the tribe of Levi, "Slay every person who helped make the idol."

Every Levite took his sword and killed about 3,000 people. Then Moses' wrath settled down. He climbed Mount Sinai again and the Lord God gave him two other tablets just like the first ones.

After he descended this time, his face glowed with a powerful shine. God gave him a veil to cover his face as the people were afraid to approach him. He could see through the thick veil but they couldn't see his face. Again Moses gathered together all the Children of Israel and recited God's commandments.

The next section of the Bible goes into directions for building the tabernacle, the curtains, the ark, the candlesticks, the priest's clothes, their breastplates, the altar, and the hanging for the tabernacle door. I, Methuselah, am most interested in the colors they were to dye the linens with since I like blue, purple, and scarlet. I think it's interesting that they used shittimwood which is a hard, heavy dense wood that grows in the Sinai desert. It has nothing to do with the first syllable. The measurements for each of these items are given, but I don't like math, especially cubits, so I won't repeat the details.

When the tabernacle was set up, Moses put the Commandments into the Holy Ark. They had a party like you never saw—with fragrant sweet incense, singing, dancing, eating, and giving thanks to God. The glory of the Lord filled the site.

The Children of Israel packed up and went on their way. Hur helped settle his wife on their donkey. "I hope we get to the Promised Land soon," she said.

"We will, dear. Remember that just when the caterpillar thought her world was over, she became a butterfly."

I, Methuselah, have related exactly what happened in Exodus and I trust you will remember that it was Moses who invented toilet paper, golf, a "brella," and other things. I hope that you'll be duly appreciative. I want to emphasize above all, that Moses learned a little from his Anger Management class in Egypt, even though he frequently denied that. His classes with Professor Abraxas may have been more important than anyone can imagine in giving him the skills to deal with the incessant complaining of the Children of Israel on their way to the Promised Land.

So long for now! See you in Heaven when you arrive.